Acclaim–

Chris Kelso

—'Come into the dusty deserted publishing house where mummified editors sit over moth-eaten manuscripts of books that were never written . . . anyone who enjoys the work of my late friend William Burroughs will feel welcome here with Chris Kelso.'
—Graham Masterton

—'Sparky, modern, avant-garde but accessible, Chris Kelso's book is reminiscent of the most successful literary experimentation of the 60s and 70s, the sort of work that was published in the later New Worlds, but it's also thoroughly contemporary, intimately engaged with modern life as it is right now. Kelso steams with talent and dark wit and his blend of anarchy with precision is refreshing, inspiring and utterly entertaining . . .'
—Rhys Hughes
***author of* Mister Gum**

—'This emerging journeyman of the macabre has wormed his way into my grey-matter and continues to seep noxious ichor. I feel like I must devour him. Every little bit of him.'
—Adam Lowe

"Chris Kelso's writing is like a punch to the gut that forces your face against the page. The way his gritty prose carries his imagination is like a bar fight between Bradbury and Bukowski, with the reader coming out on top. The worlds he drags us into are so damn ugly that you have to admire their beauty."
—Chris Boyle of *BizarroCast*

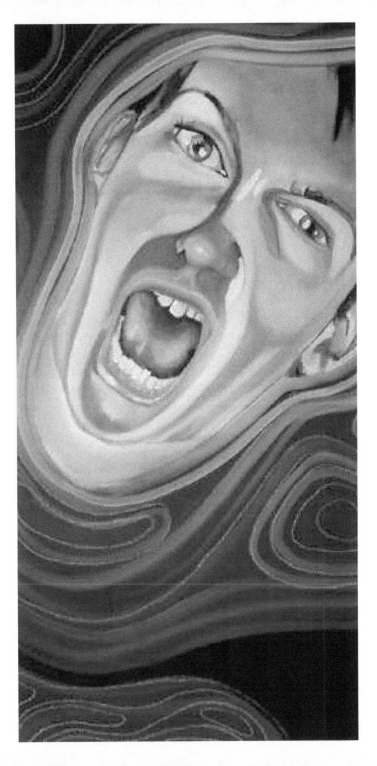

Bizarro Pulp Press

Moosejaw Frontier
Copyright © 2013 Chris Kelso

ISBN-10: 0615854362
ISBN-13: 978-0615854366

Printed in the USA.

interior layout by Lori Michelle
www.theauthorsalley.com

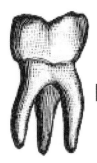

MOOSEJAW FRONTIER

Chris Kelso

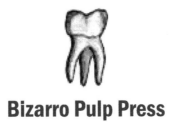

Bizarro Pulp Press

Internal illustrations by Chris Kelso

Screaming Nihilist by Vikki Hastings

Photography by Blair Dingwall

INTRO

(Thank you!)

Attention: *If you hate the following—meta-fiction and pretentious weird-for-the-sake-of-weird developments/ all intellectual masturbation/science-fiction plot devices/and if you detest the thought of an author being so narcissistic that he'd include himself as a main character in his own novel—then please skip to the last few pages of this book where you will find a genuine heartfelt apology waiting for you. For everyone else, consider this your thank you and read on . . .*

—Writer

Main Characters

Juan—*the protagonist*

Chris Kelso—*the feckless writer-man whose first novella was a postmodern denouement and Pynchon-esque meta-tale of spliced narratives intended to outline the inscrutable interconnectedness of the universe . . . it was also an unmitigated failure. He is also a pretentious wanker.*

Tamarin Bell/Professor McLeod—*the literary hierarchy*

Raymond Hogg—*a real writer who penned* Bucolic Musings in the Snake Lair *but who was argued out of existence by a radical network of revolutionaries, mail artists, poets, performers, underground 'zines, cybernauts and squatters. Hogg's name became a nom de plume for the movement who denied he ever really existed in order to take credit for his work.*

The AD-JECTIVES—*a group who informally adopted and shared Raymond Hogg's work. It was used by hundreds of artists and activists all over the Slave State and the Americas since the first failed emancipation. The pseudo-name first appeared in the town of Moosejaw when a number of cultural activists began using it whilst staging a series of urban and media pranks and to experiment with* *new forms of authorship and identity. The multiple-use name spread to other Slave towns and cities, such as Wire and Shell County, as well as countries outside the Slave-zone such as Austria-Germany, New Catalonia, and Soviet-Asia. They waged a guerrilla warfare on the cultural industry, ran unorthodox solidarity campaigns for victims of the Slave State's censorship policies, repression and, above all, played out elaborate media pranks as a form of art*

PART ONE

ONE

1812

JUAN NURSED HIS septic neck wound. People in the town of Moosejaw watched him stagger over the open-range and ignored him once he appeared on the dirt-road. The spring-loaded rattler that had risen from an innocent coil back in the Eden Shale Hills was a real beaut, in fact it was the shiny ingot hide of the beast that attracted him to approach it in the first place—but the subsequent measure of venom it injected Juan with had left him roaming the outback a delirious zombie. Curiosity could be a deadly thing in the naked ergs of the South.

He had been travelling from coast to coast in an effort to fulfil dreams of Manifest destiny. He'd moved across the Appalachians into western Pennsylvania and areas of Ohio, Tennessee and now Kentucky, but had yet to settle.

Eventually Juan collapsed in a heap outside a saloon. A man who was smoking a thin brown cigarette on the porch got up and motioned towards him. The man's name was Elroy, a Card Sharp of distinct authority.

- You all right there son?—Elroy had a fleck of cold light in the grey of his eye.

Juan moaned. A trapper called O'Neil had taken an interest and by the time anyone thought to get Juan some medical aid, a good chunk of the town was gathered around him, muttering gossip and hateful speculation.

- A French fur trader?
- Look at his skin, ain't no Frenchman.
- Hispanic? A wrangler most likely.

O'Neil crouched down to Juan's level and asked:

- You're a Hispanic?
- Yes.
- You're brave to come here when we're in the midst of a war.
- I . . .
- You heard the victorious news of our own Andrew Jackson's and William Henry Harrison?
- No and I don't care.
- The Indian savages have been eliminated.

Juan spat onto the sand. There was blood in his sputum.

O'Neil primed up another brown cigarette, lit it and sucked on its cylinder. He held the smoke in the hollow of his throat. His expression was indignant.

- I don't like your tone.
Juan smirked—I'm not selling it.
- Get the nigger some water.

TWO

JUAN FELT A stony surface beneath his cheek. He lifted his head, saw the metal bars and knew that the townspeople of Moosejaw had thrown him in prison. Juan climbed to his bunk and realised he was no longer fevered. There was an X shaped scar on his neck, he traced it with his finger. The engorged tissue looked terrible but Juan was too overcome by relief to let it bother him. Juan also had a nasty gash on his forearm.

- You ought to put a tourniquet on that arm too—said a rough voice from the adjacent cell.

The inmate was a scrawny figure with a handlebar moustache. His chaps were a piecemeal of torn leather and for some reason he still had his lariat hooked around his belt.

- I'm Craver.
- Juan.
- It isn't easy for a slave trader these days, not since Jefferson's Louisiana Purchase came along. You a Spaniard?
- Sort of.
- Sort of? Well is ya or isn't ya?

- I'm from a colonial settlement up in El Paso.
- Ha, what a place.
- Will they let me out of here or leave me to rot?
- If the folks of Moosejaw didn't let you die of that snake bite then you probably gonna live.
- Why are you here?
- Came here and got in a scrap with some filthy Indian. I won't be in here long, but I'd be lying if I thought the same for him . . .

Craver made a gesture to a figure in the cell next to his.

- Chief Sitting Bull over there got me inta this mess.

The figure rose slowly and came into the light. His sallow skin was streaked with deep cracks. He was shirtless but in good shape.

- You killed my son—Sitting Bull revealed after a moment of dramatic hesitation.
- I didn't kill your fuckin kid you redneck! It was Tamarin Bell, I told you that a million goddamn times didn't I?

The Chief humphed and receded back into the shadows.

- Lousy bastard . . .

Juan sat back down and tried to ignore the searing hot pain in his neck. Craver was still eyeing him up and down.

20

- I gotta say, your style is a little, what's the word?—
forced?

Juan became instantly indignant.

- What?
- Well shit son, if you wanted to be like the white man
so much, you be smackin of desperation.
- You people copied your style from Mexican vaqueros
and the heirs of Andalusia cattlemen.
- Oh, so you think I copied this style from the likes of
you? Some bottom dwellin, scum sucking, two-bit
wannabe white man? You is startin to irk me boy!
Now don't think for one second that the folks in
Moosejaw will side with you if I crack your skull open
with an apache axe, cos lemme tell ya, they won't!

Juan decided not to talk to Craver anymore and
lay out on his bed. He dare not sleep, because you see
Juan was a man plagued by chilling and vivid dreams.
This explained his perpetual travelling. But, of
course, there was no escape from the alternative
personality he was cosmically bound to. Sleep was
something he could never run away from . . .

Chris Kelso

The Omega-Point

Juan & Das Schloß

The wind fingered the drapes. Juan stared at his own oblate face in the window glare. He was shocked to an inner stillness by how ravaged he'd become. These dreams seemed so completely and unquestionable real.

The TV buzzed on a dead channel of static noise behind him. The glow from the screen struck certain areas of the darkened room with triangles of electric colour. This world was so ugly, so alien to him. He knew he was not the man who belonged in this world, and yet he was driven by impulses which were undeniably his own, impulses that only ever surfaced when away from places like Moosejaw.

He was having a crisis of reality—I know I exit, I know I do . . . —he told himself, rocking back and forth to the sound of car alarms and nocturnal prostitutes traipsing through his neighbourhood. This state was an effect of time travel—Chrono-neurosis; trauma to the ventral premotor cortex instigated by repeated leaps through time. He knew this somehow, despite having no idea about it.

He felt that in the past he'd taken this body to the doctor about it before.

Unfortunately, he didn't have the time to sit around and go stir crazy like this. He had got a job to do, a man to find. It was just so hard to concentrate when he couldn't even be certain if he existed or not.

Day had arrived but Juan didn't know it. A swarm of flies were blocking out the light from the sun. Juan had often been haunted by memories of a familiar and unfamiliar woman . . . someone close to this body . . . his ex-wife who left him. She had the same face as a girl he'd loved in Moosejaw called Herriot. She was the daughter of a bison herder who hated blacks. In this incarnation, his ex-wife was a querulous, small, Jewish-looking woman with cropped hair and small breasts. He loved her a lot, something in him suggested that he still did.

His Alert Watch beeped and information materialised on the screen—JUAN/HOGG, RAYMOND/NEW MEXICO/2040/CODE BROWN

He knew what it meant. Juan rubbed lotion into his drum tight skin. The haze of heat reinforced his brains cognitive sluggishness, adding to the unreality of every object in the room. Could he well afford to travel time in this condition? He didn't really have much of a choice.

---

* Code Brown is the most serious of commands issued to a TD. Whoever the TD is hunting down must be killed. This is the only necessary information disseminated in such an instance.

RAYMOND HOGG

- *Mr Hogg, are you there? Mr Hogg . . . ?*

The man Juan was after, one Raymond Hogg, was collecting his papers frantically. He looked remarkably like Juan in his original incarnation— Hispanic skin, pinprick eyes, mousy hair. Juan and Hogg were also linked, travellers of the same spirit but of a different body.

He knew someone was after him—a language cult called AD-JECTIVES. Hogg didn't know it yet but he had more dangerous pursuers to worry about. Since his new cut-up manuscript was published by a small New Mexican Press, Hogg had received nothing but hassle. He grew paranoid, swore he could hear the buzzing of another active line during phone conversations. He had since ceased all communication with the outside.

Hogg lived in an apartment in Taos, Neo-Mexico. To make ends meet he worked as a journalist for the Albuquerque/Santa Fe Journal, so everyone knew who he was in this area. Hogg was a freakishly tall, lean man, just like Juan, with strict policies on human interaction. If he weren't so intelligent you'd swear he was an imbecile.

So committed to the chemistry of alienation was Hogg, that he deliberately took a vow of silence. He hadn't spoken in over 3 weeks. He noted the strange effect this imposed behaviour had had on him both physically and mentally. He had retreated *internally, almost completely. His mouth was dry and his throat scratchy—the way any organ must respond when deemed redundant by the host body. Hogg had lost his taste in music and he was dead to the cultural curiosities of an artist. He was certain these strange changes were a direct result of his mute state. Hogg was almost afraid to talk. His own voice would echo in a terrifying foghorn throughout the apartment, cracking windows, fracturing vases, causing ear drums to explode and eyeballs to become distended.*

Hogg lit a cigarette and looked at the pile of his published books. He came to a dossier he didn't immediately recognise called Memoirs. *It had an FBI case number and a picture of him on the front (though it could've been a picture of Juan). In a strange moment of impulse, Hogg decided to pick the books up and throw them onto the crackling hearth fireplace. The* Memoirs, *he kept. He was determined to eradicate a part of himself. Even to Hogg, these changes were unexpected.*

The language cult had taken a particular interest in his experimental novel Bucolic Musing in the Snake's Lair. *All of Hogg's previous published works had been met with nothing but derision from critics and the public—but it seemed these AD-JECTIVES were quite taken with his most recent release. They believed that the nonsensical content (created by quartering old, unfinished manuscripts and re-arranging the pieces) had some hidden interpretation. They didn't seem to understand the cut-up philosophy—that the content wasn't designed to make any real sense and had no purpose beyond text manipulation and collage (and a little laziness thrown in too—Hogg couldn't actually finish any of these old manuscripts).*

* *Bucolic Musings in the Snake Lair* published by Subterfuge. It had been translated into English (British and American), Spanish, German, Dutch, French, Portuguese (Brazilian), Danish, Polish, Greek, Czech, Russian, Turkish, Basque and Korean.*

His large Roman nose sniffed trouble on the horizon, a forced entry of some kind. An assault on his personal space was as intrusive as hijacking Hogg's own thoughts. He tossed everything onto the hearth, watching each leaf of paper become a singe of wilting black fragments. He could never return to this apartment, not ever. He had to leave.*

THREE

JUAN WOKE UP in his cell. He was saturated in sweat and he had an erection. O'Neil the trapper was standing on the other side of the bars holding a notebook like someone holding a dead mouse by the tail before their naughty cat. Juan gripped his cover over his groin area.

- Just what in the Jesus St Christopher Christ is this, huh?

Juan sat up on the edge of his bunk and rubbed his eyes with the heel of his hand. O'Neil had a face of such utter bafflement that it was almost twisted into a scowl.

- Where you say you're from again boy?

Juan tried to make out the notebook O'Neil had. The sheriff appeared beside him, his expression equally confounded. The sheriff was a short stout man with mutton chops and shuffled around like someone afflicted by a bad ticker.

- This book . . . this *nonsense* is disconcertin' to say the least son. This is the ramblings of a complete psychotic. What do ya have to say for yourself?

Juan saw the cover, it read *Memoirs*. The people of Moosejaw must have taken it from him. Truth was, even Juan couldn't explain the notebook. He woke up after his first hallucination and the book was just sitting there open on his bedsit with an entry already inked in.

- I don't know what that is?—Juan lied lamely.
- Oh you don't know what this is? You hear that Mr O'Neil, the boy don't know what this is? Well, that makes a damn sight more sense than him confessin his sheer, unbridled lunacy, don't it?

The sheriff grinned a knowing grin and took the notebook from O'Neil. He licked his thumb and found a page.

- Shall I read you an entry from this mysterious diary Mr Juan?

Even though this was an open rhetorical question, Juan still protested with a silent widening of his features.

- Ahem . . . 2037, "*I wake up from bio-stasis. Here is my recounting of the experience in astral hell . . .* "

***

"*I first died in 2012 you know?—For the first time anyway . . .*

I remember . . .

The subway dawn grew dim with shadow until the rail track disappeared completely into it. Growls echoed eager in the lonely station, the flavour of the street—gone. Things clattered inside the gaping subway tunnel, things unseen, sunk deep in ink, dragging my over-active imaginations into realms of awful possibility. I was in 2037 on a personal visit—a woman actually. It ended in tears. As the midnight train heaved along its metal artery somewhere in the near-distance, I knelt to tie up my sneakers. A *BING-BONG* came from the announcer Tannoy and, after a pop of static, a nasal voice declared that the midnight train was off-schedule—fuckin typical. Although the woman I was on my way to see would not return my feelings, I became anxious that I'd keep her waiting. Only the night wind spoke once the announcer turned himself off. I clenched every part of myself capable of clenching. In the spirit of this mounting fear, I allowed a fart to skid out in the silent platform. The loud rasp ricocheted off the stone walls and echoed out, breaking the quiet like a sledgehammer. It came out louder than anticipated. I looked around to double check I was definitely alone.

I was."

The sheriff flicked over a few pages, as if all this blathering were too much even for a man who'd seen as much as the sheriff had seen.

- Blah, blah blah . . . here we go!

" . . . *a man out of context. People like me never survived in scary situations. They almost never overcame the psychological impact of scary ordeals. Ordeals sent us crazy, made us hostile and self-destructive, reclusive and scarred beyond repair. We were what made trauma funny, the ass of every taboo joke. We died scary deaths. I was just a no-body with a ridiculous name. The silence seemed to whisper—you're a dead man Juan. Am I Juan?*

I clutched my jacket into my chest, upping the collar to hide behind it. Carefully, I leaned out to see if there was sign of an oncoming train—nothing. Without even really being aware of it, I'd started mumbling.

—*You'll be ok Juan . . .*

It was odd to have solitude in one of the city's busiest stations. Then, I suddenly became conscious of my age. I don't quite know why. By this time I was almost 50. I thought everything was out to kill me. I'd die of a caffeine induced heart attack, discovered face-down in my full English with one hand still clenching a rigor mortis boner by some pack of nosey journalists (further reports would reveal a grotesquely swollen prostate, riddled with cancer and early signs of dietary related diabetes swimming through dead nerve endings).

In my teens, when obsessed with all that was bleak, I had the standard adolescent mortality crisis. Everything was pointless. I liked it in a way. But then I found some vague imitation of happiness with the big TWO-OH then slipped back into my original moroseness soon afterward. In my teens I knew one day I would probably die and only ever used it as an excuse to be sullen and pretentious. In my 20's I just sort of forgot about it, embracing adult youth and eventually—women. I married young, Herriot. But now in my late 40's I was beginning to feel death as more than a mere inevitability that lived far off in the distance somewhere, but I actually FELT death close by. Death had an interest in me—Juan— because I was closer to death than I'd ever been before! My life was grating to a halt, but it wasn't in the silent station at the hands of ghouls or ill-health where my life ended. It was, in fact, under much more heroic circumstances . . . "

The sheriff folded the notebook over and looked up at Juan.

- Juan, you said your name was Juan?—O'Neil pressed.
- Yes . . .
- So this just happened to be on your person? A memoir about someone-*ELSE* also named Juan?
- I suppose so, yes.

The trapper and the sheriff turned their backs to the prisoner and whispered conspiratorially.

- Ok, son, if that's how you wanna play it. We'll see you in the mornin'
- Wait, you can't leave me here!
- What you mean we *can't*?? You a goddamn intruder on the town of Moosejaw, not only that, you an honest to god insane person!
- I can explain!
- It don't look like it son.

Juan sat back on his bunk and conceded defeat. He really couldn't explain it, none of it.

- We'll be calling the local nuthouse to come pick you up tomorrow. Sit tight till then you crazy sonofabitch. Mr Craver and Chief Sittin' Bull will keep you company till then.

O'Neil tossed the book of memoirs into the cell.

- Wouldn't want you to miss a diary entry.

Craver waited till they had both gone and stuck his head through the bars and into Juan's cell.

- Hey, freakshow?

Juan looked up instinctively.

- Can I take a look at yer book?

Without saying anything, Juan picked up the book and forwarded it onto the eager wriggling fingers of

Craver. He snatched the book and tore it open like a kid intercepting a love letter.

- Holy shit . . . you're completely fakakta!
- Sure seems that way.
- Where's St Claire's Infirmary?
-I DON'T KNOW!—Juan was on his feet now. The constant ridicule was taking its toll—I have no idea ok! Not a clue!
- The people of Moosejaw are gonna hang you for this, you know that right?

Juan sat back down hopelessly.

"St Claire's Infirmary

. . . Outside autumn flared

. . . inside, the sound of bodies on pushcarts barrelling through emergency doors

And nurses shouting STAT

And important shoes clip-clopping on linoleum . . .

I hate hospitals. I'd only ever been to one once before and even then my reasons for being there were hypochondriac at best—I got prescribed codeine for a crick in my neck and received a kick up the backside for my inconvenience. By now my brain was more or less Swiss cheesed so I figured the health service had rightly decided there was little else they could do for me. My presence on the stretcher now garnered barely a cursory glance from the staff that came back and forth to serve other patients around me. When a doctor eventually did come over to my bedside it was only to shine a light in my eye and confirm I was, supposedly, now a vegetable.

I can hear the awful birds outside, the Winged Shaver Gangle. Their squawking, good Christ . . .

His face looked grim, I remember it distinctly.

The tan complexion he probably picked up on sabbatical in Mexico, went almost completely pale with a morbid reality. With the sleeves of his lab coat rolled up to the elbow, the doc folded both arms finally and nodded to his nurse standing somewhere off-shot.

The eager young intern dressed in bloody scrubs who'd originally been assigned to help me upon first admittance, sobbed behind the curtain opposite. This new, more experienced doctor had all the indifferent qualities that make for an efficient, emotionally withdrawn man of medicine—two dead insect eyes like piss holes in snow, a bulbous hook nose and one hand idly fingering at his stethoscope. He was chewing on a triangle of dry toast and dropping the crumbs all over my empty shell of a body. I could just picture myself in a humiliating ass-less overall, breaded like a scotch egg. I'd heard surgeons were morbid creatures, crass and always conducting their business with tasteless humour, but this doc was staring death in the face and even he couldn't hide that fact. I could tell. It was glaringly inevitable I would soon be dead. Something in my gut flip-flopped.

Since I'd arrived here, wet with blood and gibbering nonsense in a semi-conscious state, my condition had only deteriorated under the hospitals care. I'd slipped rather suddenly into a coma. I knew all about doctors. How they'd BUFF a patient just so they could be TURFED to another wing of the hospital in order to free up more beds. As a foreigner I was an obstacle of St Claire's all-American revolving door policy. That's not racism, it's merely fact. My ex-wife Heriot read The House of God. *Doctors didn't care about me, none of them did.*

If I'm honest and fair though, my overall health had been in swan-dive long before I got shot seven times in the chest trying to prevent a Poughkeepsie grocery store stick-up. My ex-wife used to go on about me giving up cigarettes and marijuana.

- Why do you need to do it? She'd ask, throwing her arms in the air theatrically, and I'd reply
- Cos it feels good, that's why!
- Good?—She'd spit with a face of strained understanding and disgust
- Yes! It relaxes me!
- Where would we all be if we had your attitude?
- Probably feeling good and relaxed I bet!

I guess she got the last laugh. That was before my hallucinations of course, before I drove her away.

Of course the real reason she left me was the coming of the Jack-the-Rabbit 500—a vibrator with an artificial personality. It complimented her, said "I love you" and if you put an egg in it, the damn thing could boil or scramble it in 3 minutes. How the fuck could I compete with that? That's when her attention began to wander. I bought her it for us both. Often I'd be too drugged up or mind melted to make love to her, not that she was honestly interested anyway, so I thought this thing might actually help satisfy her on that level. Eventually she left me for a Terra-5 Zumba instructor called Keith. Men from that planet have insane genitalia apparently— enough to pole axe you . . .

Monday

I could see a food tray on the chair to my left with an untouched hospital meal on it and a sprig of broccoli pronged on the tine of a fork. The nurse tried to feed me once I'd been deemed fit enough to eat, but the excruciating pain turned off my appetite like a light switch.

My neighbour in the ward was an Icelandic photographer called Ollie. Poor Ollie was bald from chemo and well into the latter stages of bowel cancer. He told me about Reykjavik and how he'd been left a widower 5 years previous and how he used to love, love, love eating sheep heads **(Sviðasulta!)**. With a sort of asinine grin, Ollie told me he never had an idol. Then he died. I was in too much pain to care.

The young intern tried to get me to sign my own post-mortem which, even at the time curled into a foetal ball, I thought seemed totally unethical. I didn't sign it, so they sent in this scalpel jockey to try and pull me out of the coma so they could proceed with an autopsy (cos I have no immediate next of kin). He zapped me with defibrillator paddles and murmured something about me being "barely fuckin' responsive like a total prick". My silence offended him, like someone who's just picked up the phone after incessant ringing only to receive waves of dead air in response and they're left screaming hello? H-e-l-l-o? H-E-L-L-O?, back down the line in futile frustration.

I could tell by the smell of the place I'd been admitted to St Claire's. All the doctors had a kind of continental look to them. Patients went berserk around me, tearing open their shirts and beating at their chests with two fists screaming—KILL ME ALREADY! Those patients who weren't going crazy lay horizontal and motionless on beds like dehydrated corpses—most WERE dehydrated corpses.

As it happened, the biting odour of death was stronger in St Claire's than seemed reasonably acceptable for a government funded institute of care—so the place stank of failure as well as death. It was one of those old fashioned institutions dedicated to the bowel run of the working class, unfortunately their

39

facilities were of the poorest standard and were frequently overlooked for additional funding on the grounds that St Claire's was located in such a crumby part of the city.

Had I been shot in my time I'd have been easily treated. How ironic . . .

The quack looming over me with his torch looked like a mash-up of famous politicians— he had the chops of Nixon, the global birthmark of Gorbachev, the thin, slicked black hair of Spiro Agnew and the shrunken posture of Henry Kissinger. When he stood over me I didn't feel safe under his care, his finger seemed to hover above the OFF switch of my life support machine. I probably wasn't ready to die . . .

Swooning in and out of consciousness, my mind began to wander. When I woke up in 3 minute intervals, I would occupy my thoughts with the memory of people who'd made my life a little more worthwhile. I'm not talking about family, of course I'm not! No, my pointless existence was made bearable only by a select few individuals whom I'd never even met.

The week before I got shot, I was watching The Exorcist III and I began thinking about the late, great George C Scott—one of my idols—DEAD—without ever having met him or even given the chance to thank him for allowing me the pleasures of *his acting talent. Although, by that stage I knew I was a goner and was even fantasising about being reunited with my deceased heroes. I thought about what Ollie the Icelandic photographer said about dying without any idols. To me, this was more chilling than witnessing Ollie's eventual demise choking on a round of his own vomit.*

I wanted to thank all the others too for their contribution to my very small, very mundane time on this planet. I was filled with fear and sadness and love and this seemed like the best way to get it out. It was either that or beg one of the interns to bring me a syringe full of potassium and inject me with enough of the stuff to kill me silently, instantly.

So, in my hospital bed, every three minutes when I woke up in agony, I'd begun composing mental thank-you letters to those I felt most deserving. The most obvious and saccharine being to my parents—dear mum and dad, thanks for meeting in that disco all those years ago and hastily jumping into bed together unprotected, the result was me, your own little anxious, awkward ball of flesh and bone. Thank you for the encouragement, shelter, milk, sexual repression, for embarking on a hideous, loveless marriage yadah, yadah, yadah . . .

Now I can get sentimental . . . "

FOUR

JUAN ATE HIS bread and drank his water. He was still hungry. Chief Sitting Bull didn't seem to eat anything. His tray sat outside his cell until the sheriff came by to collect it at the end of the day. The Chief seemed to drift off intermittently into these delirious daydreams. He would mutter in tongues and his eyes would reel to the back of his skull like a man possessed. No one questioned the Chief on this however. They just let him do his own thing.

The opposite cell with Craver in it was completely silent now. Because of the poor light in the prison, Juan couldn't actually see much of anything either. He got up and tried to see through the darkness. A voice came from the cell with the Chief in it, it said—*He's gone.*

Juan didn't understand.

- What'd you mean he's *gone*? How can he be gone?
- That book.

Juan was certain it was the Chief who was talking, but his voice sounded deeper.

- I don't understand, have they taken Craver away to be sentenced?

- That book . . .
- What about the damn book??
- That book is not wholesome.
- How so?

The Chief suddenly clammed up and went back to humming his indecipherable incantations. Juan could see the red cover of the *Memoirs*.

How was he going to explain Craver's disappearance to the sheriff?

The notebook was just within reach so he stretched his thin arms through the bars and pinched the edge as tight as he could. Once he had it in his hands Juan started flicking through the other entries. Juan was disturbed by a thumping noise. Chief Sitting bull was using a jack-knife as a drum stick and the back of his hand as a snare. Blood spurted out in red springs, but he made no utterance of pain. Each beat was more vicious and penetrating than the last. Juan feared the Chief might soon punch a hole right through his hand.

Through the steel bar cylinders of his cell, Juan saw the townspeople gathered in a circle. There was much commotion as a bag-headed individual was raised up onto a wooden podium. The man was limp and wet with blood from the waist down—they'd obviously broken his legs. He could make out the vague shape of the sheriff who held one end of a rope in his hand. Juan knew what was coming next. He had to get out of here before they dragged him out in front of the Moosejaw population for a public execution. Juan wondered if the poor sap being hanged was

Carver, then he heard the townsfolk chanting a familiar name—"KILL THE WRITER MAN! KILL CHRIS KELSO!"

He returned to the notebook . . .

"GIL SCOTT-HERON
Everybody' Got a Pistol

I got as far as Gil Scott-Heron before my heart eventually stopped. Hovering above a body in the opposite ward was the ghost of an African-American attorney called Zeke Carver, formerly Zeke Rivers (but he changed his name after the race riots in Detroit). He was a real nice fellow as it happened. I noticed on his earthly body, wounds resembling Jesus fresh from the cross. Zeke confirmed to me that he had died of stigmata but I'd overheard nurses talk about self-mutilation in relation to an eating disorder so I didn't completely trust his story in the beginning. He didn't seem all that distraught to be dead. He told me his doctor was a bourgeoisie flunky and his death was inevitable. That kind of cold rationality didn't suit him cos Zeke had one of those faces that exploded with joy and love for life (even in death!). His smile was infectious and his bellowing laugh more so. That he was unconcerned by his sudden, unjust evacuation from this mortal coil betrayed what I initially liked most about the man. Maybe he was an optimist in the extreme! We got to talking, my mind still preoccupied by idols and Gil.

- You know for the longest time I'd been uneasily aware of the absence of black role models in my life.

- Shit man, there's not a white person today I look up to.

- When I thought about all the people I admired, they all seemed to be white European! This wasn't consciously acknowledged by me until much later in life (I'm embarrassed by how late I left it).

- Didn't they teach you history in fuckin' Moosejaw?

- Sure, I respected Malcolm X but never thought twice about Islam or Marxism. I appreciated Martin Luther King and William Baldwin and Nelson Mandela but only through the sieve of popular media, shaking images of these men in front of me like a knot of shrunken heads. I was beginning to feel like an ignorant racist, so I dug around and was glad to stumble across some real diamonds hidden away, people who would later go on to eclipse the large majority of my Caucasian idols in fact!

- Well shut me up.

- It began with Son House—a blues singer/slide guitarist from Detroit who was part of the whole delta blues, gospel music boom of the 30's and 40's.

- I know Son House you dumb-ass.

- He had this song called "Death Letter" that I was obsessed with for a while, do you know it?

- What a question! Do I know it? . . . no.

- *When Son sang, he seemed to shamelessly wail each lyric like a kid who'd just lost his momma. When he spoke about death it was as a bereaved family member, when it was about heartbreak he sang as a distraught lover. This sort of raw emotion gave his music a particular resonance, something beyond punk idealism or your average rock n' roll agenda. It was personal music, relatable music. You felt like an eavesdropper who really shouldn't know a person that you've never met so intimately.*
- *You realise that guy next to you died of the worst kind of cancer?*
- *There's a best kind?*
- *Ha, I guess not.*
- *It's worse he died having never been inspired by someone or something. It's kind of sad.*
- *Son House would've written a great song about him in 12 bar blues.*
- *I don't know where Ollie is. I mean, how come we're here and he's not? He's just a corpse with no procrastinating spirit hanging around.*
- *No life left in him I guess, nothing worth sticking around for. We got lots to chew over, you know?*
- *As a young, impressionable, highly sensitive kid growing up in an economically depressed town (who got dumped by girls every time he was foolish enough to put his heart on the line), Son House was the only person who could ever understand me. Or at least that's how I felt for a while.*

- And from then on you liked black people?
- You make me sound like a clan member or something.
- Relax honky.

A hot nurse, whose face held pleasing symmetry, leafed through my wallet, checking my MasterCard was real by biting down on it then pocketing three unopened condoms. I realised quick that I didn't have much use for material objects anymore, so I let the hot nurse rob my corpse without grudge.

- From there I got more into artists like Stevie Wonder and Marvin Gaye.
- I guess they're ok.
- Inner City Blues *was the soundtrack to my life for over a month and as a huge fan of Gaye's version, I thought I'd see how other black artists covered it. It was here I found Gil's version.*
- It sucks.
- Well, it wasn't anywhere near as good as the Marvin Gaye original but I was still curious to see what else this new smooth, black voice could do. When I found Reflections, *I was a Gil Scott-Heron fan and forgot all about sexual healing.*
- Reflections *is ok.*
- On Reflections *he also covered a Bill Withers song I was fond of that was probably better than the original.*
- Now you're just talkin' straight up shit.

-*With Gil came politics, and an interest in something which bored me before. Gil Scott-Heron, like Alasdair Grey, Chris Petit and all the other 20th century polymaths like him, succeeded in a variety of different mediums and didn't merely excel in the field of music. Gil released two novels—*The Nigger Factory *and* The Vulture. *He was a popular spoken word poet and unlike countless others who shone brightly early in their careers, Gil did not burn out with age and undo all his previous great work. He was seen by some as a sort of black supremacist and I'm sure Gil himself wouldn't exactly denounce such a label. What with me being whiter than virgin snow, I guess you could perhaps forgive me if I were to tell you that my fascination with Gil Scott-Heron ended with music and literature. You'd be wrong though, because he was a fine man.*

- Are you really trying to educate a 46 year old black man from downtown Detroit on the history of black culture?

- I don't want the illuminate to separate me from a culture that isn't white. Gil himself would agree.

- Gil would've hated you. His intention was to keep white European crackers like you out of his establishment.

- His intention, while controversial at times, was never intended to provoke violence or create isolation, he just wanted to speak a truth he felt important. Now, black culture is well integrated and every little suburban frat

boy claims to have been influenced by Tupac or Puff Daddy.

Zeke's interest was diminishing and in an effort to regain his attention I asked him more about his personal life

- So, stigmata huh?
- Yup.
- You don't seem the religious type to be honest.
- I'm not irreligious, but I don't believe in god.
- Dying sure is a bummer man.

Dying is a pretty mundane experience in truth. There was a moment of relief to be free of the physical pain I was in, and then I got a little lightheaded. This was followed by a brief flash of shapes and jagged forms of light coming quickly at me through the black, like when you stick your finger in your eye too hard. I felt a little weary for a while. I felt like I'd escaped something, coming out unscathed through the rocky roads from Jumla to Surkhet. But now where was I? Heaven? Hardly!

- So you got an idol, good for you. You thinks you're the Earle of Rochester or something? I bet you still work 9-5 and bought your wife a vibrator.
- I'm from the future actually.
- Great.
- You'll never like me will you?

- Liking people is for the living bitch . . . "

***

*Juan fell asleep with Memoirs *open on his chest. Pretty soon he was free of his cell and dragging himself through the streets of Moosejaw in the body of the Time Detective. He passed the strewn ramparts like a lobotomised idiot, a zombie taken to the streets in search of impulsive desires. He passed a bar full of screeching aliens and resisted the urge to quench an impossible thirst in him. Might as well get this shit over with—he thought, finding a factory wall with good surface area. The weary Time Detective dropped his chronovisor, drew his photonic-crystal gun and poised the nozzle around the walls middle. He squeezed his finger over the trigger—a blast of exotic matter flew forth from the tip like multi-coloured ejaculate.*

The mouth to hyperspace gaped in a swirling vortex. Juan sighed.

This was a draining journey for a Time Detective. Unfortunately mental preparation was something he hadn't had time for either.*

Chris Kelso

The newspaper today—

BARONESS UN DIES, A SLAVE STATE MOURNS (KIND OF . . .)

Crowds gathered by the barriers opposite St Raul's Cathedral, many with Slave State confederation flags, to watch Baroness Un's funeral—but not everyone was there to pay their respects. The coffin's journey caused a mixed reaction among slaves lining the streets, with some onlookers applauding as the hearse passed while others fell silent.

The procession was littered with these small protests. While there were no incidents which verged on political demonstration or acts of anarchy, the big bon voyage for the Pink Ortega Colony's most famous daughter was not without confrontation.

An ex union man Bobby Chinaski held up a banner reading "Rest in Shame" as her funeral cortège approached while boos rang all throughout Flee Street. Jeers of "Waste of money" were also directed at the band and applause further up Lumpkin Hill. The Un's Good Riddance Party Facebook group posted an invitation on the social networking site encouraging members to "time your protest with the passing of the cortege" and travel to the meeting point in small groups.

Un's apparent insensitivity to the plight of

industrial Shell County had made her a hate figure in mining towns and it seemed that even in death, no one was willing to forgive and forget. Senior reporter at The Slave-Today, John Langsyne tweeted: "As the Un funeral begins, Shell County's main civic square is deserted. This town is not for mourning."

Around 300 demonstrators gathered at Wire City Circus, at the intersection of Flee Street and Farringdon Avenue, to show their opposition to Lady Un's policies and the cost of her funeral.

Chris Kelso, a director of the cosmetics company Lush, said: "We need to represent the wide breadth of public opinion—some of us do not wish for Un to have what amounts to almost a Royal funeral. I find it distasteful that the Slave State would pay for this considering the crucial role the Pink Ortega Colony had in Earth's demise."

Un's peers have downplayed any ill-feeling. As her procession got underway in central Spittle, Slave State Chancellor Marcel Cordoba called the day a "fitting tribute to a great overlord".

Mr Henri Bastard, the leader of the coalition government, said it would have been seen as extraordinary not to commemorate her life.

"I think it will be quite a sombre event."

FIVE

THE AD-JECTIVES BELIEVED all language was a cancer. The structures of words and the restricted order of language was a prison. Put simply, they were a crazy bunch of pro-asemic cultists led by former Nobel Prize winning author Tamarin Bell. Since he reached the peak of success by age 30, he just sort of went insane. He and his group had taken to siezing unconventional literature to add to their "new canon".

Bucolic Musings in the Snake's Lair *was a top priority. Bell wanted to publish the novel under his own name and have it printed for a mass market. Bell belied that Raymond Hogg was not the true author either, but rather the conduit through which the text was communicated. Bell also believed in xenolinguistics, demiurges and all kinds of hocus pocus voodoo nonsense. He was perhaps criminally insane.*

***

Juan gave a jaw breaking yawn as he stepped from the massive time-scape gateway. He felt a little better but remained very tired. He still didn't know why he had to murder Raymond Hogg. The details were a little sketchy. Something about saving humanity or maintaining order or some such, Juan hadn't really paid attention to the brief. All that was clear was Hogg had to die.

He'd been to New Mexico before and didn't like it. There was something too familiar about it.

In no time at all Juan arrived outside Hogg's apartment building.

What a piece of shit—he thought out loud. He knocked lightly on the door to the rhyme of pop-goes-the-weasel.

- Excuse me friend, anyone in there?

Silence . . .

- Mr Hogg? It's quite urgent sir . . .

Silence . . .

- Hey asshole! How about answering the fuckin door sometime?

Silence . . .

- Last chance fuck-face, answer the fuckin' door you dumb little prick.

Juan had no problem killing people. He'd done it 6 times before (in both avatars) and after the first 2 it barely registered as anything more than work. At first he'd had reservations. That was until he got a

great piece of advice from a serial killer called
O'Neil—killing someone is the best way to overcome
a fear of death.

He reached into his great trench coat and
screwed a silencer onto the end of his photonic crystal
gun, calibrating the settings to "DISINTEGRATE". He
blasted the door and the wood began melting
inwards until there was an entry hole big enough for
Juan to fit through. The other tenants watched
through their peepholes as the man from the future
forced his way into Mr Hogg's apartment.

Juan looked around, seeking cover behind the
corner of each wall. It looked as if someone had
already broken in here. The apartment was a mess
with tables overturned and drawers open and
raided. He tried communicating again.

- Hogg? Where are you?

Juan grew anxious. Code Browns were
important, if you ballsed them up, there could be
awful consequences. Even he knew that. Suddenly
Juan heard a movement. Peering round the wall he
could see a figure just standing there. He twirled
around and did a dramatic forward roll until he was
hidden behind a centre table in Hogg's living room.
He rested the butt of his photonic crystal gun on the
glass surface and yelled FREEZE.

Juan had a good sight of the man who appeared
unarmed. He was wearing a poncho and had long
dread locks and an unkempt beard. The man stared
deeply back at Juan, no fear in him.

- *You Raymond Hogg??*—barked Juan. The bearded man grinned and spoke in a foreign dialect. The whole incident was perplexing even for someone as far travelled as Juan.

The man was Tamarin Bell. When he opened his mouth it went something to the effects of

- *Affababababalalaaaalllalaterraherraballaba!*

Juan stood speechless. Everything seemed twice as surreal as before. For a few moments he and Bell stared intensely at each other until Juan asked where Hogg was at.

- *You'll never get to him before we do.*
- *And just who the fuck are you?*
- *I'm hurt you don't recognise me.*
- *Aye well, cry me a river . . .*

Bell looked at Juan high-tech weapon and was so unfazed by it that the TD was actually intimidated.

- *I can tell we do not share a similar ideology. When the Omega Point comes, we are all that will survive.*
- *If you don't start talking sense soon I promise I'll shoot you in the face.*
- *The supreme point of complexity and consciousness. I can see in your eyes an absence of some sort. You have a nonlocality to you. Have you ever thought of becoming one of the enlightened?*

Juan stood up and, momentarily, allowed the photonic crystal gun to drop by his side.

- *You mean, have I ever thought about joining a visionary cult?*

- Yes . . .
- Honestly?
- Yes . . .
- No . . .

Juan brought the gun back up, cocked it and told Bell to put both hands on his head.

- You are not a policeman. Even if you were, you have no authority. You are bound by conformed linearity. Even your native language is a stifling burden.
- Ok that's it, last chance, were the FUCKIN HELL is Raymond Hogg?

Tamarin Bell stepped towards the open apartment window. He grabbed a fistful of his poncho and for a second Juan thought he was reaching for a gun. To his surprise, Bell rips the poncho open at the chest to reveal a t-shirt reading "AD-JECTIVES—THE COSMIC MIND". He started getting up on the ledge.

- Get down from there you crazy cunt!

Bell climbed onto the edge and stands up. He produced a match and struck it till a small flame starts to flicker.

- I've enjoyed our dialogue—he said calmly.

Bell raised his hand with the match in it and set himself on fire. The last thing Juan heard him say before the awful sound of crackling flesh was something about "Long lives my cosmic mind!"—Or words to that effect. Bell eventually lost his footing and the flaming cultist plummeted 10 stories to a gory conclusion on the sidewalk below.

- Fuck sake . . .

Juan was angry and more confused than he was in the beginning. What was so special about Hogg's manuscript? It seemed to have a reality distorting effect of its own. People were behaving in crazy ways to obtain it. This case was exactly what he didn't need. His reality crisis returned with a vengeance. Juan tried to clear his head but the intrinsic doubt in him was overwhelming. He went over to Hogg's refrigerator in the hope of finding alcohol. Instead he found a bare cabinet with a jar of teeth stuck in the salad crisper. The jar was labelled—covert listening devices.

- Crazy cunt . . .

***

Hogg had devoted a certain part of his brain to matters great and profound.

A part-time cosmologist, part writer, full time cynic—this was all the information you could obtain, or indeed ever need, when conjuring an image of Raymond Hogg. His brain was concerned with limited things, although the paths ran long and winding. Now Hogg had to try to concern himself with a new paranoia. A man who has not laughed or cried or sang or uttered a word in so long is as close to insanity as Juan. For poor Raymond

Hogg, a writer and a mere husk, he was truly doomed. You almost sensed that these two men were kindred spirits although both were much too stubborn to ever realise it. Hogg cooked up a drug— a solution of tap water and opium stuck in the gauge of a no.26 needle. He spiked himself and every muscle in his body relaxed. Hogg fell asleep between the narrow walls of an alley.

In the morning it was his plan to hitchhike a ride on the Pan-American freeway. The world around Hogg had become alarmingly hazy. Everything appears twice removed. Hogg dismissed this as validation of a tired mind.

***

The police arrive at the scene soon. A band of spectators gathered around the decimated corpse of Tamarin Bell. He was lying in bits all over the sidewalk, bust open like a bag of meat. Night time had set upon the city. Juan was growing impatient. He couldn't stop thinking about the Omega-Point. He wanted to survive, even though he knew this event (if it had been rightly prophesised) could not happen for years, even ahead of Juan's own time. However his inability to advance into future time-scapes left an element of doubt swimming around his head. He didn't like spending too long in past climates either.

His Alert Watch buzzed but he didn't look at it. He knew it would be Fairfax or someone calling in to see if Hogg was history yet. It occurred to Juan that this unreal state of things could be more than just Chrono-

neurosis. Perhaps he had failed to prevent Tamarin Bell's legacy and this dream like state was an effect of the Omega-Point trying to snatch his consciousness from him.

Suddenly he saw something—a ripple in the air which undulated into a torrent of distorting waves. Juan's first thoughts were that a vortex was forming. Maybe the rest of the TD's were on their way to help. But then a woman emerged, naked. Her dainty features obscured by a hideous scar covering one half of her cheek, like markings of a flourishing continent on a globe of the Earth. She approached Juan slowly until there were only inches between them. He placed his hand on the perfect oval of her face, running his index along the delineations of her scar. He recognised the woman, though he knew her when she was much older. He'd recognise his wife's face anywhere.

- We can be together again Juan.
- We can?
- In a superior state of being, of twinned consciousness . . .
- What happened to your face?
- The fleshy vessel is a delicate instrument. It is not designed to re-form after the Omega . . .

A third eye blinked open on her forehead. It didn't look like her other two eyes. There was no kindness or humanity there. Juan was disturbed by the difference, he saw her as infected by a parasite. She was blemished like a reanimated corpse, cobbled together by a mad scientist. Juan was struck by an overwhelming desire to see this terrible imitation die.

- You're not my wife. My wife left me for Dylan

Thomas. Why wouldn't you want to share consciousness with him?

The eye on her forehead arched angrily.

Before she had a chance to react a blip sound tore past Juan's left cheek and landed a pinprick sized hole in his wife's forehead—right between the eye. The eye ball oozed a green slime but she didn't seem in too much pain. Juan turned around and saw Chris Kelso—a fellow Time Detective and a royal wanker.

- Juan, get away from her!

Juan stepped back instinctively. Kelso moved closer to the alien replica of his wife and raised his photonic crystal gun.

- Get back in the wormhole bitch.

Juan's wife sniggered, not a feminine snigger but the victorious cackle of the antichrist. Kelso didn't hesitate. He blasted a final shot into her chest and booted her back through the portal. He shot another round directly through the wormhole and it closed immediately.

- What the fuckin' hell is goin on?
- The Omega-Point is a crock of shit. Tamarin Bell was victim to outside influences not of this world.

Juan looked at Kelso and saw everything he loathed in humanity. There was nothing worthy of respect. Juan was from the autodidactic mould where people learned things by themselves. Kelso was the opposite of this principle, he was an over educated tit who's dad was a Glasgow Calteck benefactor. What a tit . . .

- And you can prove that can you?

- The Omega-Point is a trap, that's all it is. They lure people in with promises of eternal transcendental life, but when they enter the portal all they experience is slavery! Do you know how many people we've lost to the bogus Omega Point?

- No.

- A lot! We've lost so many good detectives to this thing, didn't you read the memo?

> *Juan noticed something affected in Kelso, a haunting memory of the sheer wholesale loss of life.*

- The memo was far too brief! I didn't have a clue what the fuck was happening.

- Did you actually read Bucolic Musings in the Snake's Lair?

- Of course I fucking didn't!

- I think you'll be surprised when you read it . . .

- Do ye now?—Juan said confrontationally and no less intrigued.

- Yes.

- I didn't get Hogg . . . —Juan conceded with an element of self-reproach.

- He's been picked up somewhere in Roswell. We found him hitch-hiking out in the desert.

- So Code Brown is complete?

- Almost.

- What else is there to fix?

- We still don't know who's behind the Omega trap. We've spent years trying to figure it out.

- Why was I chosen? I'm crap at my job.

- I don't want to say you were expendable Juan . . . but, well, you were.

- Great.
- We know that Hogg's book has something to do with it. These beings are trying to kill humanity through art. It has a big influence on us. These beings know they can trap us with it.
- So is Hogg one of them?
- Don't know. He could've just been a host body.
- Couldn't we just go back and kill Hogg's grandfather or something?
- There would be too many repercussions. The literature he wrote before his cut-up novels prove hugely influential to the wellbeing of the world's future state. The governing TD body would never allow us to eliminate one of the Slave State's greatest exports either. He's loathed right now but in a couple of years, well, you know how important he became.

Juan nodded though only to save himself from appearing stupid. In truth he had no idea who Raymond Hogg was prior to this mission.

- Raymond Hogg is a crucial part of our nation's tourist trade! We had to get rid of him around the time Bucolic Musings in the Snake's Lair *was written. We need to destroy the book, but with those bloody AD-JECTIVES skulking around, destroying the final manuscript could prove problematic.*

Juan was trying to forget the sight of his wife. Although he knew perfectly well it wasn't really her he just saw, the sight of Chris Kelso shooting her in the chest has incensed him.

- We found a syringe of pure 20th century heroin on

him. I thought you might need it. I know you've been having a bit of a head-fuck recently.

Something wasn't right. Chris Kelso was as straight laced as a TD comes. He wouldn't condone hard drug use, especially the strong stuff from this century. Everyone knew about Juan's addictions, why would he abandon his ethics and exacerbate the dependence of a peer?—Because everyone hated Juan?

He snatched the needle from Kelso anyway giving a distrustful glance. Kelso begun revealing details about Hogg's heroin.

- It gives the user an incredible sense of abeyance, a true Dadaist's drug.
- Sounds a bit dangerous. You tried it?
- Oh yes, you enter a kind of touch sensitive reality. It's very freeing.

Kelso caught sight of his own reflection on the greasy bonnet of a parked car. He stood gazing into it proudly, like Narcissus entranced by his own image in the reflecting pool—a devoted and long serving slave of Nemesis. His attention returned to Juan.

- Go on then. Give it a go.

Juan was hesitant. The warped mind-set hadn't dulled his instincts. Then again, he knew he couldn't turn down a hit. He thought about Hogg, about how he never asked for any of this. Juan felt an alien emotion wash over him—compassion. Hogg was just like Juan. People just wouldn't leave him alone. All he wanted was to have a bit of peace and quiet. He tried bending the rules and it only got him into more trouble—a slave to the world around him, trapped by his own context. Juan handed the syringe back to Kelso.

- It's fine. I can get my own drugs.
He noted the choked disappointment in Kelso.
- Fair enough I suppose. After all we've been through I'd have thought you could trust me.
- Unlikely mate.

Juan walked away from the crestfallen TD. He picked up his photonic crystal gun and downed his Chrono-visor.

- Where are you going?—asked Kelso.

Juan blasted a hole in the street wall and turned around.

- Do me a favour, give me some peace, huh?
- Peace? You're a Time Detective you nonce! You don't get peace!
- Well I'm done with this case, and I'm done with you! Find another expendable officer to do your dirty work and take your dodgy heroin.

When Juan looked into the vortex he'd made he saw the fabric of the universe. The wormhole resembled the Omega-Point. Anything could feasibly lie beyond this location. The closest he'd had to unified consciousness was with his wife, but now that was gone. Alien slavery, repressed state apparatus/ ideological state apparatus, other modes of government deception, a bunch of cultist nut-jobs, malevolent unified conscious or worse, a life of unhappiness and mental illness in his own century . . .

Juan yawed and walked on through . . .

PART TWO

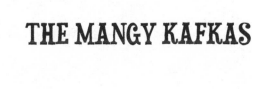

THE MANGY KAFKAS

SIX

—*"This kid is a plagiarising moron with a fascination for all things scatological, and not in a good way! As if that weren't bad enough, he is sometimes compelled to include ME as a character in his nihilistic little yarns—the long prick of coincidence? I think not . . . "*
—William Burroughs

—*"Chris Kelso is a talentless hack . . . I hate him and his shitty books . . . "*
—Amazon user, LUVZTOFUX

—*"I hope Chris Kelso gets HIV in his anus, I don't know if you can actually get HIV there but if you can I hope he gets it!"*
—Ghandi

—*"Chris Kelso's work makes me feel young again, reminds me of when I was 18 . . . and couldn't write worth shit . . . "*
—Ernest Hemingway

74

—*"The man's work is an exercise in self-referential hogwash. He is the sole reason why I had a vasectomy."*
— **Gordon Kelso (father of Chris)**

—*"I'm not implying Chris Kelso has a tiny penis, but if his stories are anything to go by, well, he better have a good personality!"*
—**Sigmund Freud**

Chris Kelso

The Mangy Kafkas

Somewhere in the dark bosom of the highlands, Professor McLeod—the nation's foremost creative writing scholar—was resting his feet atop the strained backs of two failing teenage undergraduates. Their backs quaked under the weight. McLeod was marking his student's latest assignments—they all seemed to have failed miserably. *At first*: the buildings shimmered beneath the glowering crimson sun satellite. This was the way it had always been—eternal light, warmth intrinsic, purity assured by any means necessary. There could be no night; it was not permitted, served no purpose. Each columned high-rise appeared antiseptically clean, sterile and stainless to the point of featurelessness. This was the way it had always been . . .

The castle where he taught stood on a mantle of rock, dangling over a cliff edge near the Hoag Islands. A giant mouth embedded in the ground below waited for morsels to jump. Students would oft go to the precipice and let their legs hang over, staring dead eyed and brain-weary into the crashing saliva surf beneath.

Professor McLeod had a strict policy on suicide— if you were forlorn enough, and so compelled, then acts of suicide had to be performed quietly and after the midnight curfew.

McLeod wandered into the classroom, first period, with a bag of groceries in his arms. He sat the bag on his desk and pulled out an orange. Professor

McLeod had an old face with the look of borrowed flesh, scored deep by time with divots and creases. He peeled away the rind slowly while the students waited in silence. Once the skin had been shed, McLeod plucked the orange apart, before placing each segment into his mouth. He chewed with his mouth open and made the most obscene noises, almost deliberately. Once the entire fruit had been consumed he dusted his hands indicating that class was about to formally begin. McLeod pointed at a boy, a sad, ashen faced creature hiding a metal gum-shield beneath his frown; a boy who needed sadness to maintain a human form.

- Kelso, your assignment was garbage.
- Yes sir . . .
- You weren't able to tame the characters at all. You should've known Juan wouldn't trust you or take your drugs. Do you care to explain yourself?
- I was trying to play with a familiar and overused story arc . . .
- And failed!
- I am not a very good writer Professor McLeod.
- No, you are not, but that's the point of these classes isn't it? I can make something of even the most useless brains.
- I suppose sir, but I'd rather do something else now.
- Meaning, you do not want to write??
- Yes
- Well, what would you rather devote your time to?"
- There's a job going as a shelf-stacker back on land that I'm thinking of submitting a CV for.
- Thinking of submitting a . . . ? The only thing one of my pupils will be submitting is a manuscript to a literary journal!

- But professor McLeod, I'm really no good. I have nothing interesting to say. I'm a fraud, don't you understand? In all your time teaching this course, can't you see that I'm a damned fraud??

- I only see a young writer too afraid to commit to his characters.

- No sir, it's not that at all. I have released a novella and a short story collection, both within a month of each other. They are of limited availability in small book stores. My Amazon reviews have been mediocre, my friends and relatives provided the majority of the positive ones. No one has bought them, no one will review them. As one Amazon customer, who was not a friend or family member stated, 'this writer is a fraud of the highest calibre'. If a man with an account name "HALLEBERRYSNATCHSHOT" can see that I'm a no good phony, then why can't you?

- Writing is your calling, is it not?

- Yes . . .

- Then you have no choice but to stay here, do you?

- But professor, I need to make money. My books won't sell, I'm not that type of writer. I don't appeal, even in the underground my books are unknown.

- The underground is a bigger place than you think Mr Kelso.

The boy thought for a moment then realised that resistance was pointless.

- Your book was a failure because you gave up.

- I . . .

- You need to go back to your aborted bastard story and resuscitate.

***

Kelso held the book *Memoirs* in his hand. Professor McLeod had given everyone a notebook to jot down any sudden inspiration which might fall upon them, Kelso's was empty. His one entry read— *Sometimes I can't believe how much I hate myself, everything about me. Looking in the mirror makes me sick to my stomach like I wolfed down a bad clam or something. I actually **get** why people would dislike me. Sometimes I want to fuck my head with a boulder; I'd smash it till my skull and face completely caved in. What a way to go. It'd be great to see my own funeral. I don't want people to show up so I can feel sorry for myself one last time.*

Nothing struck him as profound or potentially engaging since signing onto McLeod's course. The long midnight jump from the precipice was growing ever more tantalising.

The necropolis on the hill past McLeod's castle was a veritable advert for both Merchant capitalism and the burial custom of the Scottish antiquity. These days it was filled with students corpses. Grey sheets of rain were blowing all the way through the grounds while brassy sighs and groans emerged from air-breaking buses grid-locked outside the gates. Brollies shot up making sloshes from wet plastic. Along some granite blocks on each adjacent side, a grotesque gargoyle monument gave its once over to all that rested beneath it. Both horns were iridescent, the block of its torso corroded by rainwater, freckled by tiny motes of light and its bronzed gonads swung like two creamy green avocado pears. An intersecting Celtic cross bearing angels of hope, charity and faith were gilded in Mercury, carved and cast in ceramic, copper, tin. Marble busts convened, hoisted upon plinths at the side of the great pyramid of the mausoleum with its grand proscenium archway sculpted in spelter. Below the hill, rows of unmarked Plebeian graves had been ruined by quad bike vandals, sitting crooked alongside urn fields and tumulus mounds of earth, stone-age cists, toppled headstones, and a series of collapsed chamber cairn arrangements. Indifference was the essence of McLeod's teaching. The gargoyle scrutinised large Equestrian statues, a Thinker in sober meditation, all of which were framed by gifts of wildflowers from the children of Wishart Street. A student called Raymond Hogg came running up to Kelso. Once he caught his breath he started smiling widely and went straight into it.

- Chris, have you heard?
- No, what's wrong??
- It's McLeod, he's dead!
- What?
- Yup! Charlie saw a Gangle attack him!
- A Gangle??
- A bloody great big Gangle! The Gangle started tearing him into a shredded blur of homespun tweed apparently.
- A Gangle has never attacked a human before.
- Well, it sure knew how to pick the right bastard for his first attack! You know what this means?
- We're free?
- Free as a Winged Shaver Gangle!

The Winged Shaver Gangle— a native to the Moosejaw, this formidable waterfowl scavenger normally feasts on brine-shrimp and gather near the mudflats and wetlands of the city's coast. Moosejaw has become a famous tourist destination as a direct result of the birds colonisation here. They have proven to be good, loyal pets, bearing many exploitable characteristics which are advantageous to the human populous. Such advantageous features typical among the Winged Shaver Gangle are— Along its chest are ruffles of multi-coloured plumage that can change colour to acclimatise with its environment which are cut and used as fabrics for clothing; It's pink bill is a whopping 19 inches long and can skewer difficult to reach fish from the rivers making it popular among trawlers; It possesses a unique dentition—lethal, fanged cusps that are packed into broad triangles along the ridge of its mouth. The Gangle achieves flight via an airfoil shape wing structure with leading cross section and limb bones that are lined with razors (hence the name). The bird has fore-limbs that are able to propel it through the air at speeds of up to 70 miles per hour. While they aren't known to enter the city's public space, they are always audible as a consequence of their eerie, goose-like honk. Their meat is a nourishing, if slightly taboo delicacy, although it is not uncommon that the owner of a Winged Shaver Gangle consume the flesh of the bird when it has reached the age of 7 years old.

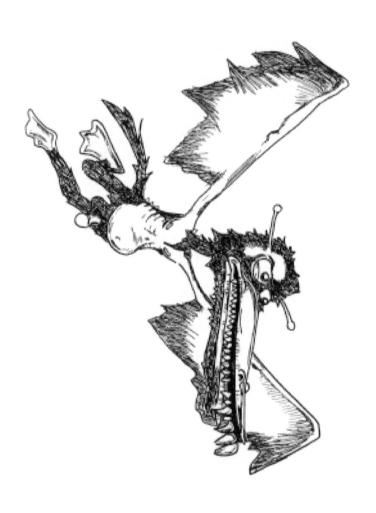

Now: a twisted shadow dawned in front of the sun's globe. Before long it had achieved an eclipse and the darkness prevailed, vomiting the most awful ink blackness over each structure compiling the cityscape.

A man's head rolled down the immaculate, onyx streets. His flesh was scorched at the cheeks, his traits generally eggshell-frail. The head belonged to Juan. Kelso held the head without a body in his hand. He observed the dull features, the cancelled eyes of nothing, the bashed, hollow skull concave where an intelligent mind may once have throbbed. Still it didn't feel real, there was something so innately unreal about the character of Juan. He just couldn't bring the man to life. Juan's conception was a mistake in the first place, he was a deformed ugly, unrealised child and Kelso hated him with every ounce of his creative spirit.

Kelso tore through the vicious night without a trace of fear in him. Now that McLeod was dead he was free to do what he wanted. He could finally get that job as a shelf stacker. He thought about what he'd like to do with his life. It occurred to Kelso that he did in fact harbour a deep desire to be something in particular—a clown. He'd enrol as soon as possible. Prancing through the streets in a state of ecstasy, he wore a raggedy brown dress buttoned tight around his throat. He had donned a large sun hat (in spite of the absence of any actual sunlight!) which displayed an artificial daisy tucked into the band. Around his shoulders were the cart of jars, light glowing from inside. Kelso also had a basket of light-filled gherkin jars loaded into a wicker basket which he carried around by its wrist loop. Time to sell his dreams. He'd sell them for bargain prices. Anyone who wanted them could have them! The jars clunked together. That's how people knew he was coming. Kelso was sunburnt because he refused to wear the protective masks—he felt they overwhelmed his physiognomy, and so stuck to wearing just his great, floppy hat. Once his last hope and ambition had been sold, he could finally start his new life . . .

SEVEN

ELROY DISENGAGED A shell into the newly fertilised yolk of a Gangle egg. For a card sharp he was a pretty good shot. O'Neil the trapper stood watching over his shoulder.

- Don't want those mother fuckers spreadin'!

Having persuaded local engineers to lend and use their equipment, the drainage of Moosejaw's wetlands was the first port of call. One local contractor even made available his own customised machinery, free of charge—Concrete pipe machinery to be more specific. He called it a Centrifugal Spining Compressor which would effectively split the sea bed like a chain trencher then fill the watery gap with granular material which would then be pumped into a large septic sewer trap.

Everyone watched as a cluster of Winged Shaver Gangle's conglomerated on the lowland bogs, fighting, fornicating, and filling the on-looking Moosejaw folks with more disgust. A chain of newly hatched egg shells sat poached, runny with embryonic fluid near the sea. Even O'Neil had to stifle his gag reflex.

The sheriff signalled to the contractor to begin reverse irrigation of the birds swamp. Then with a wave of his fat hand, gave the word for those with automated artillery to start taking out as many Gangle's as they were able. Elroy was the first to release a shot, exploding a white male's skull into pinwheels of blood. "HONK, HONK!" The birds were squawking and darting aimlessly in alarm. None of them tried to retaliate.

When the last shell had been withdrawn, the carnage of Gangle corpses littering the lowland were flounced slowly away by the gradually thinning sweep of remaining tide.

As soon as the coast was finally drained of all fluid, no one could quit believe what was left in its hollow grave—what else, but a gaping **mouth**.

***

Juan sat on the edge of his bed. Chief Sitting Bull was so silent in the opposite cell all that could be heard was laboured breath. The townspeople had left in their droves over an hour ago. Juan was becoming increasingly desperate and frustrated. He was sick of being trapped, not just inside his cell, but there was a feeling that even if he achieved his freedom that a greater prison awaited. The snake bite on his neck started pulsing again.

Around this oral pit, a series of laterally faced, rotted teeth lined its upper pallet. The stench of a warm breath attacked the people of Moosejaw. Elroy rested his gun on the floor and stepped to the overhang. Peering down the canal of its oesophagus, the moist highway of a tongue wriggled, wet like a slug. The mouth must've stretched back over 20 miles. Stuck in the canyons of its teeth, dangled the cadavers of numerous butchered Gangle birds, some of which had only been wounded and were flailing about and honking. It was obvious to everyone that the rest had taken the long, dreadful journey down the abyssal throat. O'Neil noticed a pulsing ulcer on the left expanse of gum. Almost instinctively, he retrieved his gun and aimed it at the haemorrhage, but the sheriff threw his arms around the weapon, snatching it from the trapper.—Are you a damn invalid son?

Suddenly the ground shook. The coast land begun to crack and separate, morphing the mouth into a new shape. It wanted to talk.

- BE GONE THIS THIRST !—A powerful voice deafened the humans on the shoreline. The voice was important, rolling consonants with grand intention. The city-folk were frozen, clenching every muscle not yet fatigued from massacring.
- WATER!—It was now painfully clear that this mouth, whatever its source, had been feeding from the ocean.
- I TASTE THE BLOOD OF MY HOLY ANIMAL

Elroy panicked—Oh Lizard Christ! What have we done? We've upset the lizard god! We killed his Gangle! Were done for!

- I AM TAMARIN BELL!
- Who?
- TAMARIN BELL! BUT I ALSO GO BY THE NAME MCLEOD! KEEPER OF THE COSMIC MIND, ACHIEVER OF TRUE DIETY STATUS! A SACRIFICE FOR THE LIZARD GOD!

The voice continued to boom. O'Neil's curiosity had now turned into fear. One man, a baker, was fidgeting with the shank of his gun. The shirt he wore into battle had been removed when the joy of killing got too much for his sweat glands. He wanted to say something but kept biting his lip. A triangular bush of pubic hair peered through in wispy tips from beyond the equator of his waistline. Eventually he gave into agitation.

- Well you're the holy one and all! If you're so holy then just smite one of us down.

Taking confidence from the baker's audacity a local merchant poked the sheriff with his opinion.

- You heard the mouth, it wants a sacrifice!

The sheriff could see where this was going. There was no loyalty amongst the folks in Moosejaw. He pleaded with the mouth

- What kind of sacrifice oh powerful mouth?

A moment passed and the coast remained twisted but still. Then suddenly

- I WANT ALL THE MEN TO COME FORWARD!

All the men took a big step back. O'Neil and Elroy shared a glance as the shoreline crevice rumbled, breaking further afield, fracturing the earth beneath them.

- Bring the mouth the nigger!
- Yeah, offer up the nigger! He's fuckin insane!

***

O'Neil came bursting through the prison doors. The second he locked eyes on Juan, Chief Sitting Bull stood up.

- You comin with me Nigga!

O'Neil frantically sought out the key that unlocked the cell door. Once he found it he immediately stuck it into the keyhole in a way that suggested all the unwholesome proclivities behind the Trappers dark stare.

- Don't try nothin fancy boy.
- Where are you taking me?

Juan was genuinely concerned he was going to be hanged like Craver and the writer. O'Neil grabbed a fistful of Juan's collar and manhandled him out of the cell and into a pair of cuffs. He led Juan into the town square, through the battlefield of Gangle corpses. When they came to the chanting crowd of people, Juan heard the awful voice.

- LONG LIVE MY COSMIC MIND!

The townspeople of Moosejaw had started reciting

the words along with the great gaping maw. There was a sense that they had no real idea what they were chanting about, but the fear in them was so great they were slaves to it. There is no man so servile as the man who has witnessed god . . .

- LONG LIVE THE COSMIC MIND! LONG LIVE THE COSMIC MIND! LONG LIVE . . .

When the crowd saw Juan they stopped reciting. He looked over the edge, into the great mouth and for 5 minutes or so (maybe even longer than that!) just stood there in complete silence. Then, Juan's neck started puckering, breaking the skin into fractures. A gaping mouth formed. It spoke to Bell in the secret language of the AD-JECTIVES. The people of Moosejaw couldn't believe their eyes.

NECK:—AFFFALABABANNNAJJJALA BELL.

(TRANSLATION—TAMARIN BELL? YOU RUINED MY LAST STORY.)

BELL:—ABAFNNA DONKOO?

(TRANSLATION—HOW SO?)

NECK:—OABAFAL DISWALLA BON AFALABI AFFFIIELLEIJSJXJDH K

(TRANSLATION—I RAN OUT OF PLACES TO GO WITH YOU. I THOUGHT BY KILLING YOU OFF I COULD TAKE THE STORY SOMEWHERE INTERESTING. I WAS WRONG. I LOST MY MAIN CHARACTER AS A RESULT.)

BELL:—BAASGYGDS HGS HGSYGYUGG GSGSDK

(TRANSLATION—SURELY THAT IS YOUR FAULT, NOT MINE)

NECK:—EGGA MANKSIPALA DIES FAULT PROFESSOR

(TRANSLATION—ACTUALLY, IT IS YOUR FAULT PROFESSOR)

BELL:—KELSO?

(TRANSLATION—KELSO?)

- Speak English—Juan's neck hollered. The mouth embedded on the basin of the sea yawned. It's breath smelled like rotten feet, the soles of which had been dragged through fields of garlic and excrement.
- VERY WELL!
- YOU KNOW THAT IN A LARGE WAY YOU ARE TO BLAME . . .
- HOW TYPICAL OF A STUDENT! YOU CANNOT DEAL WITH THE FACT YOUR CREATION HAS MORE OF AN IMAGINATION THAN YOU DO! JUAN WAS ABLE TO IMAGINE HIMSELF AS A REAL PERSON, SOMETHING YOU COULD NOT DO. HE EXISTS IN THIS WORLD, HE IS FLESH AND BLOOD, HE DID THAT HIMSELF, INSPITE OF YOU! IN MOOSEJAW HE IS A FULLY REALISED HUMAN BEING. THE CHARACTER YOU INTRODUCED INTO THE WORLD WANTED TO EXIST SO BADLY HE KNEW HE'D HAVE TO TAKE MATTERS INTO HIS OWN HANDS AND DO IT HIMSELF. EVEN JUAN IS FULLY AWARE OF HIS CREATORS MISGIVINGS AS A GOD!

Kelso had nothing to say. The huge mouth said one final thing

\- GO TO MY STUDY AND FIND YOUR CASE STUDY. I'VE MAN-MANAGED YOU FOR MONTHS . . .

ZONEKILLER

EIGHT

Zonekiller

KELSO UNLOCKED THE door to Professor McLeod's study. He found a scathing article the professor had written about the first novella. After leafing through a stash of underage pornography and a diary of plagiarism confessions, he came across a file with the title *Bucolic Musings in the Snake Lair*. Kelso recognised the name. When he opened up the file there were reams of rejection slips. McLeod had ruthlessly itemised and graded Kelso's work and kept print-outs to catalogue his failure.

Chris Kelso

- Dear Chris,

Thanks for submitting to Foxtrot.

On this occasion I have decided not to use your work. Due to time constraints I've had to resort to these rather unhelpful form letters; my apologies for being so impersonal. I appreciate your interest in Foxtrot Books and wish you the best of luck placing your work elsewhere.

Best wishes

- Dear Chris

Thank you for sending us a chapter of your novel McDonnell's Skeleton Orgy. *I'm sorry to disappoint you, but we are unable to consider it for publication. Do try other publishers though. We're publishing only a very small selection of fiction, starting next year, so we are not accepting much just yet. I wish you well placing the novel elsewhere.*

Best wishes

Chris Kelso

- I'm going to pass, but it's an interesting premise and I appreciate the look.

- Dear Writer

Many thanks for your submission; and please excuse the impersonal nature of this response—but the volume of submissions we receive makes it impossible to tailor personalised replies.

This is just a quick email to acknowledge safe receipt of rejection.

Chris Kelso

- Dear Writer:

We regret that the manuscript you submitted does not fit our current editorial needs. Thank you very much for thinking of us! Please try again.

Regards,

- Hi,

I'm really sorry about the long delay getting back to you, and also sorry that I didn't notice that your story is well outside our guidelines. All stories for Subterfuge must be of about 500 words or less. Please don't hesitate to submit anything that might fit our guidelines, and that isn't complete horse manure. Please visit our website for more information. Who are we kidding . . . you're story was shit . . . I mean REALLY shit . . . monolithically shit . . . SHIT SHIT SHIT SHIT SHIT SHIT . . . .

Ooroo for now, Love Declan A

Chris Kelso

- Thank you for submitting to Purple Panther Lesbian literary fiction magazine. *The editors read your work with interest, but in the end, decided not to take it for publication in the magazine. We are sorry to send a disappointing reply and wish you every success with your writing.*

Yours sincerely,

- Dear Chris: Your submission "She" has been withdrawn from consideration from Skinny Letter.

Chris Kelso

- Hi Chris, These are a 'no' from us.

Cheers

- Dear Chris,

Many thanks for submitting your stories to Cellophane. As a very small press we have to be extremely selective about which books we decide to publish and unfortunately these don't look right for us. I think you have some good ideas and wish you every success with placing your work elsewhere, but we need to be highly convinced if we are to take something on. Thanks again for considering us.

Yours sincerely,

Chris Kelso

- Dear Chris,

Thank you for your interest in Kozia. I'm afraid that this story is a bit one-note: a long-winded complaint ended by a deus ex machina. For this reason, I won't be able to accept your story for Kozia.

Seamus Melrose Editor

- Chris—

Thanks for sending Skeleton Orgy *my way. I'm afraid, however, that the story isn't quite what I'm seeking for Jerry's Load, so I'm going to pass. Our poetry editor, Aaron Turner, will be in touch regarding "The Iron City" and "The Uncanny Valley." But I wouldn't hold my breath.*

Doug Bradley

Fiction Editor

Chris Kelso

- Hi Chris,

This economic downturn has hit the independent publishing world hard. As a newer publisher we've had an even harder time than most. Because of this, we are not taking on any new writers at this time. We wish you good luck in finding a publisher for your work.

Sylvia Prentice

McLeod's brutal cataloguing of every rejection letter was part of his attempts to own each pupil's mind. Kelso figured the professor probably had a filing cabinet for every student. He remembered a book he read at university, *Against Therapy* by Jeffrey Masson that painted psychiatrists as vampires who fed from the dark thoughts and precious intimacies of their patients. McLeod was a perfect illustration of this idea. The cover also had a profound impact, displaying a professor with hollowed out eyes, a column of prison bars lining up and down the socket where inside a sad-faced person in need of treatment was imprisoned.

Kelso rummaged through the drawer some more and found a voodoo doll with a large crochet needle sticking out of its head. An array of strange feelings swept over him—the first was that of abject horror, that his educator would so viciously sabotage his own students mind. As much as he detested McLeod, Kelso was bereft. This horror and disappointment soon gave way to something else entirely. Kelso experienced a new clarity that refreshed him and invigorated his artistic soul. He clenched the shaft of the long metal pin and thought about removing it. Perhaps if he managed to pull it free he could finally finish a story for once? But it wasn't as clear cut as all that, wasn't as simple as just pulling the needle free. Kelso knew that the ecstasy of ignorance was a difficult thing to recreate, especially after the creative juices had returned to occupy every waking thought. In truth, he had come to quite appreciate all those other things in life. Apart from his root obsession with the story and recapturing control of Juan, Kelso really rather enjoyed having the great albatross removed.

Chris Kelso

He really didn't *want* to write anymore. The life of a writer was a prison, absent of love or connectedness. Maybe this was what the professor was surreptitiously trying to get across? Maybe McLeod was doing Kelso a favour, trying to break his spirit by having him believe he had no new or original ideas? Then it occurred to him. He *had* to find Juan and implement him into this story, because then and only then would he truly be free of it all. One last flight! When Juan had found a home Kelso could sit back and enjoy the rest of his life—without all the writing and heartbreak. He also knew that he couldn't simply **remove** Professor McLeod's voodoo needle either. It was lodged there and no amount of tugging would ever truly prize it from its position in the centre of his skull, it would leave a wound that could never heal, a gaping hole in the brain where ideas would fall out like drips from a leaking faucet. If the needle came out then he'd bleed to death—only McLeod could remove it because only he knew how to treat the wound properly. Kelso almost regretted selling the lighted gherkin jars full of his hopes and dreams, then remembered that they'd serve only as a hindrance anyway. Now he could go on with a liberated mind. Everything up until now had happened for a reason. It felt good to know he was on the right path after all, that soon it'd all be over and he could live a life again. He realised professor McLeod was not the devil, because while the devil was intrinsically evil, he could be bargained with, and therefore, to an extent could be considered reasonable.

Kelso put the voodoo doll back in the drawer along with the rest of the files.

110

***

Juan had collapsed. A sharp gust of wind punched him in the small of his back, (although he could have been pushed), his knees buckled over and he went soaring into the air and down the long column of the mouth. The pungent aroma of saliva grew stronger the deeper down the throat he fell. Juan felt consciousness waning as he was being dragged through the vortex of his poorly realised parallel life once again. He submitted completely to it. He would not miss Moosejaw . . .

Cousin Cathy had a long, trim column arching gracefully into the aft mounds of muscular buttocks. She'd been created by the writer as a vicarious outlet for his strong sexual feelings towards an unobtainable girl of the same name. Juan, privy to the majority of his creator's thoughts and feelings, soon formed a similarly unhealthy attraction towards the notion of this girl. Kelso had written her into a story but turned out to be nothing more than the perverse fantasies of a deranged, sad and lonely individual. The broad screens of her scapula appeared to lurch confidently on its slim, clear canvas. Below a tablet of body art (an uncurling butterfly and a snake) the coin-slot crease of her ass clefted alluringly. On Cathy's ankle was a cracked heart tattoo—figurative in a sense to the hearts she must've trampled through on a recurring basis. Juan's impression of her was so strong, especially for a woman he'd never met and would never meet. He prayed that he could be with her. Heriot looked on from Quantum Hell with a tear in her eye. She wasn't based on any one person in particular; in fact the few splices of her personality which had actually been taken from people who existed in the real physical realm were obnoxious and unattractive. Heriot experienced a great urge to obliterate herself completely—which, as a fictional stock character who only ever frequented the periphery of a talentless writers worlds, was quite understandable. She felt herself dissolve into a bad idea . . .

***

The nurse looked at her patient suspiciously. Juan was hog-tied to his bed at the wrists and ankles, spread-eagled, gazing forlornly out the asylum aperture into the cosmic crib of night. He tried to scream but found himself restricted by a strip of gaffer tape.

Juan had really done it this time. While attempting to travel back in time to seduce his younger cousin Cathy—Juan, stuck in the foggy thoughts of incestuous lust, set his Alert digits to the wrong time/location. He ended up in Shell County asylum, 1982. Of course when he began preaching of his origins in the future, it wasn't long before Juan found himself banged up in the loony bin.

Now, instead of luxuriating in the taboo love of Cousin Cathy's virginal embrace, he was being sexually abused by a fat, nameless nurse.

She was a strong looking woman, hulked at the neck like cattle; the sturdy posture of a mangrove dwelling ungulate. She glared down at him. Juan could see up the dark caves of her snout.

- You've been a b-a-a-a-d boy . . .

She rested one enormous knee on the bed, tipping the balance to the left side under her weight. Juan saw the embroidered edge of seamed hosiery.

- You're a cute one aren't ye?

He felt the nurse's plump sausage fingers leech up the inside of his leg.

- Familiar with rape fantasies . . . ? Your gaffer Kelso has them all the time . . .

Juan hadn't fucked time travel up this much since he went back in time and convinced Stanley Kubrick to make Wartime Lies, *a movie which inspired Sissy Singer—the biggest murderer of the 22nd century—to gun down a thousand civilians from a department store vantage point.*

The cumbersome nurse leaned in to whisper something.

- Ever had a fantasy yourself wee man?

Juan shook his head in denial, even though he'd harboured the most unspeakable fantasies about Cousin Cathy since his infancy.

- I got a fantasy wee man . . .

The nurse ran her massive palm over Juan's skull, streaking beads of perspiration from his forehead.

The asylum walls were sallow, sickness and disease hung in the air. Juan was helpless.

- Time for a bed bath I reckon . . . hope you don't try to—the nurse grazed her thigh against Juan's fingertips— . . . TOUCH ME or anything . . .

He craned his neck to the left and saw the wall become distorted. Like an answered prayer, Juan recognised the shape of a vortex appearing in the ward. From it stepped Chris Kelso, the most noble, heroic time detective in the history of the trade. Juan had never been so happy to see him.

Kelso was tall, built and really quite strikingly beautiful in his way. He had a thick mane of well-maintained black hair and was literally the sole reason why the world hadn't yet collapsed on itself. Kelso leapt from the portal and sprinted to Juan's bedside. He took one look at the awful nurse and roundhouse kicked her to the temple. She went down like a bag of hammers. Kelso untied Juan and slung him over his shoulder. While advancing on the shrinking wormhole, two institute nurses tried to tackle our hero, but he managed to deftly hurdle them both and make a perfect jump forth.

***

Back in Moosejaw, Juan and Kelso landed outside an abandoned factory. Kelso dropped Juan to the tarmac. He was clearly upset.

- You could've been killed!
- I know . . .
- How could you get the dilation so horribly wrong?

Juan shrugged, feeling his gratitude drain to resentment. He hated getting lectured.

- *Ok Juan, if you make one more mistake you're out of the TD, simple as that. I'll stop writing about you. That means I take your photonic crystal gun and your chronovisor away. You'll never travel again, you'll never exist again.*
- *I hear you, I hear you. Jesus Christ.*
- *Listen Juan, you're going back to basic training. End of discussion.*

Juan was beside himself but quickly realised it could be the only way to keep his TD license—without it he might never get to shag Cousin Cathy!

***

On the screen, a training video was playing. It was called "So you want to keep existing?" In the cramped office cubicle, Juan sat slouched in a bucket chair with three other wannabe detectives, all of which were apparently no older than 17 years of age—no doubt a sorry band of unrealised characters themselves, typical of the human detritus which composed Chris Kelso's mind. Subsumed by regret and boredom, Juan willed the clock hand to hurry up—but he couldn't control time with just his mind alone. The instructor flipped off the screen and asked if there were any questions. Juan felt the air tear a yard behind him, as an eager trainee put his hand up.

- *So, when can we see the photonic gun?*

The instructor, a skeletal specimen with bifocals, smirked smugly.

- *No, no. You're nowhere near qualified my boy. Patience is a virtue.*

The trainee descended his hand and looked more than a little deflated.

Juan yawned and stared at his watch, making no small secret that all this unnecessary training was entirely below his capabilities. The instructor noticed.

- Do you have a question Mr Wank?
- It's Juan . . .
- My apologies . . .
- Why would I have any questions? I've been doing this job for months.

The instructor squinted behind the large orbs of his eye-wear.

-Ah yes, perhaps the rest of the class should be illuminated about your past in the service?

Juan groaned.

- Mr JUAN is a disgraced TD—a man who, on more than one occasion, has almost brought about the destruction of our planet with his misadventures. A man who thinks he is ready to become a major character. A man who has lost all bearing on his reality, who turns his nose up at his creator, who . . .

Juan stood up and approached the instructor. He thumped him with a left to the jaw then dropped a fist onto the back of his cranium. All the trainees clapped. Chris Kelso burst through the door as if he'd been waiting all along for Juan to behave this way. He grabbed Juan by the scruff of the neck and dragged him out of the cubicle. All the trainees crowded to the door to get a good view.

- Since you only understand one method of punishment, I'm going to teach you a lesson the only way I know how.

Kelso withdrew a photonic crystal gun and blasted a swirling vortex into the wall. He picked Juan up by the collar and tossed him through the shifting dimensions of time and space.

When he regained consciousness, Juan could smell the fresh purity of Cathy, of her cotton jumpers and her tousles of golden hair . . . then it gave way to something much fowler, though no less familiar. The gag ball of guilty arousal Juan associated with his cousin's youth had gone sour, travelling in an acidic up-stream reservoir from his gut to his throat.

- You ever had a fantasy wee man . . . ?

Kelso knew he'd never have to worry about Juan again. Certainly he would be haunted by his ghost which would inevitably twist and turn near the inlets of the writers mind, but he could cope with that, just about. Juan would live on as a lingering doubt near the medulla oblongata, tucked snug between a million other missed opportunities and regrets that cluttered this dank, lightless corner of skull. Kelso could practically feel the red ink of Professor McLeod's marker pen scrape an "F" over the canvas of his life. Kelso could finally do what he wanted . . .

Chris Kelso

The newspaper today -

ASPIRATION NATION V TOMORROW NEVER COMES

The Slave State chancellor delivered a confident Budget report despite mounting pressure, relentless heckling from party members in the hive and an animated response from the opposition leader.

Marcel Cordoba took to the podium and prepared to deliver the contents of the green boxes. He began candidly: "I will be straight with the state; another bout of economic storms in the Slavezone would hit the country hard."

Cordoba was quick to blame exports and recreational activities for the economy's weakness and revealed a forecast growth of 0.69, downgraded from 1.2% in December. But Office for Slave State Responsibility predicted that the UK would escape recession this year.

Amongst other reforms, the chancellor announced a big package of anti-tax-avoidance and evasion rules, which he said would send a message that tax avoiders were "not going to get away with it".

Most government departments were

predicted to see budgets cut by 1% in the next two years while schools and slave-unions would be ring-fenced.

Chancellor Cordoba said this budget aimed to support "people who aspire to work hard and get on in the State". He added: "Our slaves are important to us but if they continue to watch television, read books and socialise then it will be harder to use them for the greater good. It's a budget for people who realise there are no easy answers to problems built up over many years just painstaking work of putting right what went to badly wrong. We've cut the deficit by a third, helped business create 1.25 million new jobs and kept interest rates at record lows."

The 1% cap on public sector pay would be extended and limits on "progression" pay rise in the sector. A cap on social care costs was also confirmed.

Like schools and health, the military is to be made exempt from "progression" pay limits. There will be a single flat-rate pension of £144 a week brought forward a year to 2016.

Regarding the environment, Cordoba spoke at length. The Slave State will take forward two major carbon capture and storage projects and offer new tax incentives for manufacture of ultra-high emission vehicles.

There was good news for the unemployed

as Cordoba's report predicted that 600,000 more slave jobs would crop up this year.

Slave State Executions leader Bart Bastard approached the bench to retort. Few expected the scathing tirade that was to follow. Bastard berated Cordoba's promises for a brighter tomorrow.

He added:"All he offers is more of the same. He almost need not have bothered coming in as it was all in the Standard before he came in. We need to increase Executions for those who don't respond to Slave State letters and e-mails, not make things easier for them."

Bastard attacked the growth forecasts from the Office for Budget Responsibility which had been slashed from 1.2% this year to 0.6%. He said: "The slaves deserve better when it comes to rewarding the hard working slaves and appropriately punishing the lazy ones. Every budget he comes to this House and things are worse, not better for this State. Compared to last year's budget, growth this year down, growth next year down . . . "

The backlash came to a gruesome head when Bastard questioned the chancellor's competence.

Bastard said: "All he offers is more of the same—higher borrowing, lower growth and a more of the same Budget from a downgraded chancellor."

NINE

THE CONS OF SINGULARITY

By RAYMOND HOGG

The Vivisector

A GROUP OF *surgeons are leaning over me. I can see the narrowing dimensions of my own body laid flat on an operating table. I'm covered completely in blood. Hiding the doctors deed are blue stained aprons, paper mache'd across my open incisions. Sensible shoes are clicking along a linoleum floor. Coming into view, the doctor's hand is twitching, holding a scalpel while a nurse dabs his sweating forehead.—This man has no heart—the nurse observes, seizing the main surgeons overall in shock. The surgeon examines my exposed cavity, peering into the depths he has created.—No soul either—he finally adds. The nurse and the doctor share a knowing glance before turning off life support . . .*

If anyone was going to get me in the end, I'm glad it was me. My name is Raymond Hogg. I am the author of 25 books, although most likely you know me for Bucolic Musings in the Snake Lair *which was hijacked by a group of literary cultist conceived by Chris Kelso. I find myself here, in Astral Hell, because a writer put me here. He could not control his characters and didn't understand how to fit them into the context of their plot. I am also a creation of this author, but I hate him. I am not an atheist because I know he exists, but I do despise him for what he did. As I was being fleshed out, as I was beginning to adopt some semblance of a real person, he took life away from me—killed me off in some vague unseen plot contrivance. I hate my creator so much I wish him ill health. You see, the creator, or the author as you might know him, is a selfish man. Because his body exits in the physical realm, he thinks he is better than us. He is wrong . . .*

My problem is that I expect too much. I feel like if I mope around eventually someone will feel sorry for me, show me a little mercy. It's a refusal to change, a laziness of the soul, intrinsic, unchangeable. This is also the fault of my creator. But every pig gets slaughtered and every man is forgotten. Time has aged me in ways you cannot imagine.

I met the Hydra in quantum hell.

Quantum hell is where negative people go when they enter an astral plain. The super attractor we've all been moving towards is in fact, the Hydra itself. Where pathetic characters are absorbed into one body and forced to converse with one another until the end of infinite time.

Disconnected from the temporal world, hanging

over a balcony, Hogg pitifully observed the gunmetal gray residential buildings frozen beneath the gloaming. The Cages of brass stacked high behind ugly allotments. The smell of firecrackers hung heavily in the air but it was a smell he didn't mind. Hogg knew none of this was real. It was all he'd ever known.

Gibbous and limp with boredom he started patting down his coat, rummaging for cigarettes. He pulled out some low tars, eventually located on the inside pocket. Lighting the fag Hogg began wiping a smeared fly from the glass patio door with a tea towel. As he inhaled he pulled a sour face.

Raymond Hogg saw the Hydra—a mass of ectoplasmic muscle which dwelled in the abyss between time, absorbing brains whenever it could. Ironically, it was time travel which summoned the Hydra into existence. He was a fully conscious manifestation of dilation—go figure.

- The Hydra hasn't consumed my brain yet; perhaps it can sense the bomb still ticking away in some submerged quantum reality. He has many heads and they're all chatty bastards. One particularly annoying head called Desmond, used to be an actor from Ayrshire. His shitty personality stinks of Chris Kelso. He talks relentlessly.

- Encounters with the Ghost

I was perfect as an actor—A Jewish pantheist from a single parent family who erred frequently on gay abandon.

123

Chris Kelso

Inside London's Old Vic theatre some students, including myself, were about to receive a tutorial from the great Willy O'Hara. The same cherished actor who had starred in last year's Grand Guignol production of Glasgow Junky Autopsy *in this very theatre to universal acclaim.*

I had always been a huge fan of his. Ever since we studied his masterful execution of the Meisner technique in intermediate drama class, I took it upon myself to find and analyse every production he'd ever been part of. I thought his take on the Glasgow junky-with-a-heart raised the bar for similar style roles. And I was about to meet him! Allegedly during Glasgow Junky Autopsy's *first run, O'Hara's fourth wall-breaking monologue reduced my drama instructor as well as the rest of the theatre audience to fits of unbridled tears. Met with a standing ovation, O'Hara's junky seemed to possess unprecedented measures of depth. It's no small secret that he lived in the shadow of that role for his entire career either.*

- You have the right to kill me, but you do not have the right to judge me!—echoed O'Hara as he forced the prop of a hypodermic needle into his forearm. Wonderful stuff.

So there we were, crammed into the main dressing room like gulags, eagerly anticipating our idols entrance. Some highly strung students were calming each other with breathing exercises. Labberd milk stank out the neglected greenroom refrigerator. I thought maybe we should throw it out *but surely there would be no time for a clean-up on any comprehensive scale. Then we all gasped as a knock on the dressing room door indicated his arrival. People began chattering and fidgeting with so much expectancy. I became aware that there was still a chance this wonderful occasion could be completely marred by our own foolish over estimations. This was a seminal evening and I didn't want it ruined by expectation or pressure. But I couldn't have been more wrong. O'Hara breezed in with all the graciousness and presence we built him up to possess. All that was garden-variety about the man was his olive sweater vest. His cargo jacket yawned open to the midriff. Willy O'Hara was taller in real life and in some way better looking—he'd grown a sphagnum of facial hair that suited him right down to the ground. He introduced himself and led us all out into the main stage for our first lesson.*

Willy O'Hara walked us onto the stage, the same stage where he'd turned in yet another memorable performance as King Lear in a city production two years previous.

The stammel curtains were drawn but even the boardwalk itself gave everyone goose-flesh. O'Hara looked remote. He began denoting his disapproval towards most young drama students, informing us all how he found them arrogant, pretentious and often latently homosexual and that we too would probably be no different in his estimation. It seemed already we'd nettled him. I grew increasingly wary. But then I thought to myself—O'Hara often delivers his tirades with that blowzy, working class exasperation that had made him such an icon around these parts in the first place, so we shouldn't be too offended—except one girl named Susan who wore frumpy dresses. She was offended by absolutely everything, an individual who detested all things non-cervical.

The teacher hates his pupils as the driver hates pedestrians as the shop keep hates his customers.

- Lie down on the stage people . . . he instructed. We all complied with gusto. At this point, I was sprawled centre stage staring into the main, voided spotlight above. O'Hara had begun to weave in and around the tapestry of student bodies, stepping over heads and tiptoeing over entire torsos. It was amazing just to hear him—that voice from the television, that commanding, now disembodied, Scottish narrator whose very prized vocal chords could penetrate souls upon release.
- This is a difficult job, getting up every day, having the motivation to perform 8 times a week. You kids don't know work yet. Find ways of making it interesting for yourself, that's the secret. Trust is important. No one trusts anyone these days. Trust your fellow actors . . .

O'Hara's voice burred nicely, but I noticed he had a kind of slick L.A schwa that surfaced on certain vowels, quit possibly obtained during his short, unsuccessful spell making American independent films where he was typecast as fishermen. After this initial exercise, which seemed to serve as nothing more than an opportunity for our esteemed teacher to reveal further dislike towards our kind, the curtains were hauled up. O'Hara's face ceased its blustery intolerance. We all watched with keenness what was being unveiled, but I kept watching the unveiling of Willy O'Hara. He had suddenly become quiet and insular and on the verge of something close to tears. Sure enough, the curtain lifted to reveal the great proscenium. All the seats were lit by strobes but O'Hara told us that, more often than not, the theatre was more intimidating without the lights— at which point, almost on cue, the footlights shut off and we witnessed first-hand what he meant. In the pitch black playhouse, Willy told us an amusing story of how he once got so loaded on vodka during a show that he fell into the orchestra pit. For one nauseous moment we all thought he'd start to cry. He began to dispense intimate details regarding his past alcoholism. O'Hara was, to a degree, soliciting sympathy and we met the terms without any grudge. It looked like he'd finally warmed to us. Undiminished by our less than vocal response, Willy clapped his hands for us to start reading our lines.

- Sometimes, becoming a character can be—O'Hara paused for emphasis—rather draining

London was jam packed with people who couldn't make a life for themselves. I included myself among that category of people for the longest time. I moved here because I naively thought it would open doors. Truth is, before I was accepted by the Old Vic, I'd been incredibly close to calling it quits. I'd become drained myself by the efforts of it all. Willy O'Hara had achieved exactly what I wanted to achieve but

*looked so weary, more like I did in my early
unemployed days roaming Camden. Then he started
to talk again to no-one in particular.*

- Waste of bloody time.

*None of us really anticipated that we would wind
up his psychiatrists for the evening, ready in the
wings with paper tissues for the treatment of picked
psychological scabs and poked wounds. We'd have
to be on our game to stem the gleet. What a strange
night that was.*

*The next evening we prepared to go on stage for
our companies own rendition of Shakespeare's*
Macbeth. *Having landed a principle role as Banquo,
I was presented with a decent amount of lines to read
for a change. Willy O'Hara promised us he would be
in the audience and we all relished the opportunity
to perform in front of him. It was a privilege our
instructor told us.*

*Scene 1 begins but O'Hara isn't in attendance. I
cast it to the back of my mind, as I'm sure everyone
else who noticed his absence similarly tried to.*

Macbeth crowed

**- When the hurly-burly's done, when the
battle's lost and won . . .**

*I admit that worry had set in by Act 2. In
retrospect O'Hara might've seemed a little jolted,
even unstable during the previous night's lesson. He*

128

became something much more human—as if loathe to reveal his true intentions. My worry was to have proved far from tenuous as news began to circulate that Willy was indeed dead. No-one knew any real details; just that he'd died that very night after taking our class and would be immediately replaced by Siegfried Chopin, head instructor at Deutsches Theatre in Germany. It was really as simple as that. We were all forced to move on. With someone like Willy, you could never be certain exactly what squashed them in the end. It could be drink, it could be drugs or woman or depression. Willy was normally so personal we had no one suspicion regarding his method or reason.

No bones about it though, Willy O'Hara's Glasgow junky always did have so much depth . . .

And that's what you have to put up with! Pretentious shit talk. Still, least there's a mute to my left. I spend most evenings discussing the details of my suicide. I elaborate on the ticking bomb dormant in my skull. They all nod interested, until the conversation dries up, until it's their turn to yabber on and on and on . . .

So there you have it. The grass is NEVER greener on the other side, take it from me—I've been fuckin everywhere!

TEN

CHUCKLES STOOD OUTSIDE his apartment door—jagged perpendiculars of the rotting city visible through the lobby curtains. There were bloody claw marks dragging all across the wall and the hallway stank of something fetid. He looked down at his oversized clown feet and sighed hopelessly. There was still a gob of saliva on the tip of his left shoe. Troll-faced kids had been spitting at him all day. Mrs Wernicke walked past and nodded hello. She was covered in dirt from the factory. Sometimes he thought she knew who he used to be, but that was impossible. Even when he was a writer and hung out with writers no one knew who he was. Chuckles honked his nose.

His other neighbour, Mr Primer, was watching a horror movie on full volume again—the sound of women screaming really made it hard to get a good night's sleep. The walls were unreasonably thin in Complex-K5 and privacy was an impossible luxury, but Chuckles didn't like to complain. He slotted the key into the lock and went inside.

After removing his face make-up and bright red

nose, Chuckles sat down on the sofa and turned on the television set. The screams from Mr Primer's apartment seemed particularly loud.

Suddenly Chuckles became aware of a rustling sound underneath the strewn debris of shit in his apartment—*Another cockroach maybe?* The clown picked up an iron and stealthily sought out the source. It seemed to be coming from behind the radiator grill.

- Come out!—Chuckles demanded. After a few moments he called out another warning. The rustling became frantic and a figure emerged from behind the baseboard—a boy. He was covered in bruises and had a stare on him like a frightened animal. Chuckles dropped the iron.
- How long you been back there?

The boy cowered. He looked familiar but Chuckles couldn't put his finger on why yet. There was a sudden knock at the door and the boy dived back behind the cast iron. Chuckles told the boy to shush and went to answer the door.

A small woman with a mousy moustache was standing on the doormat. Her cheeks were stained with tear tracks. She held up a piece of paper with a child's face on it.

- My son. You seen him?

Chuckles took the picture and studied it closely. It was the boy hiding behind the radiator, there was no doubt about it. He remembered the boy's desperate expression and figured he was running away from abusive parents.

- Sorry, I ain't seen him.

The woman looked at the clown suspiciously before eventually moving along to Primer's apartment.

Chuckles closed the door over and told the kid he could come out.

- Why are you running away?

The boy kept his mouth shut.

- Ok, you can stay here till you're ready to go. There's food in the fridge.

***

Chuckles got home late the next day. He was performing at an 8ᵗʰ birthday party for a little girl with a suspiciously goblin-like face. As he reached the foot of the stairs he saw Primer. He was sniffing great nostril-fulls of the rectangular portal of his doorway.

- Everything ok Mr Primer?

The ugly old man stopped frantically inhaling the air and swivelled to meet Chuckles. He was wearing monogrammed silk pyjamas covered in dubious red smears.

- You got something in there, something I want.

Chuckles brought out his key and eased past his senile neighbour.

- Nothing in here Mr Primer . . .
- You got something, *oh you* got something . . .

Chuckles nudged past Primer's shoulders and squeezed through the gap between his door and its frame. Inside, the apartment had been ransacked. Chuckles started calling after the kid, checking under every piece of over-turned furniture. The kid was gone. The clown began to panic. He couldn't explain the paternal fears which coursed through his body and made his skull numb with dread, but he was a slave to them. Chuckles suspected Primer might know something about the boy.

Out in the landing people had gathered by front of the window. They were looking at something outside, on the roof . . .

***

The kid was clambering across the roof tiles of Complex-K5. Something was in pursuit of his supple flesh. Chuckles pushed through the crowd of spectators and stuck his head out the window. From the sound of feet frantically skittering across the slates, the clown knew the boy was in trouble. Almost instinctively, Chuckles pulled himself onto the ledge and then up onto the roof. On the opposite side he could see two figures running. As they ran under the lunar light, Chuckles was horrified to see the kid being chased by his moustached mother—only she looked different; while before her features had seemed dull and cumbersome, they were now strained wide with a rabid anger. *Why was she so mad?*

Chris Kelso

- Hey, leave him alone!—Chuckles protested, somewhat benignly. The kid's face was covered in tears and his expression of panic sank an anchor of nausea in the clown's gut. He had to do something. Quickly . . .

As the other tenants gaped on like looking fish, Chuckles had tossed a noose around the cheese-filled body of the moon. He tugged at it with all his might until eventually it became dislodged from the smog riddled skyscape. He grabbed the boy and held him tightly under his catch. Chuckles and the boy swung on the great vine until it steadied and the clown began scaling towards the moon.

The book *Memoirs* lay on the surface. The kid had jar of light in his hand. Chuckles recognised this object. He knew that somewhere else a disconnected part of himself was living a different life. The creative spirit, long since banished . . .

FINAL ENTRY—The Slave State, inside the fourth zone, inside a radioactive graveyard where only ghosts and wild animals could live, that's where you'll find me—where the damaged core of reactors 3 and 4 would eventually vomit their explosions of molten concrete lava into the neighbouring towns below. My home is the town of Shell, one of the worst infected areas after the disaster. From my room, you can see the ghostly Ferris wheel, motionless since 86. My local lodge is long abandoned and is now a sanctuary for albino deer and wild dogs. The red forests with a sparse stretch of skinny, naked pines emerge burned and rusted by cancerous radon gases.

I may be dead, but I'm saddened nonetheless. I feel as I have always felt.

Still I can see everyone I used to know—Mrs Kowalski staring forlornly from her balcony as if the world were about to end. Beside her, her husband (a liquidator) rests under the quilt, his book page folded over to chapter 11 of the book he never reached the end of. The teenagers who used to play under a bridge outside the tenements continue to do so. Only now, they fear the light of day instead of the coming of nightfall.

McLeod is still alive. He walks around the alienation zone with a digital frequency meter beeping away. He says he hunts ghosts like us. If he finds me he'll try to make a writer of me once again. I cannot go back to that. I will not go back to that. While he speaks frequently to us, we have never spoken back to him. This town is full of fictional characters and that's all I want to be now. The man who got sick of trying to be God. Why can't he just leave me alone? I'm doing my best to blend in.

The radiation seems to have little effect on his body. I don't know about its effect on his mind. Some say he came from the sarcophagus the Slave State built to contain and stabilize the void created by the power plants turbine hall explosion. Others say he's hunting those responsible for the killing of his brother who, they say, was a worker in the plant. But I know who he's really after . . .

Every day he walks through the desolate remains

of my town, stalking shadows and suspicious flickers of light. I wonder if he isn't dead himself. His world is probably as grey as ours.

Today, McLeod is starting his crusade earlier than usual. Morning has just come up. He arrives in the earlier train, docking at Shell County station. This is the only signs of life anywhere near this area before it departs back to civilisation. The dikes are over-spilling with contaminated water from the floods of spring. Mutated cattle drink from the water. I love it here. McLeod watches on hatefully. He is repulsed by the cattle. He is repulsed by this whole ugly world.

Mr Nazarenko sees him come. Together we watch him gain closer to our housing block. Through the dark corridors he dawdles like a hunter on the tail of precious prey. Admittedly his commitment is admirable. The Professor is middle aged with a handle barred moustache and a cigarette roll perched behind his ear. His face is wrenched in permanent disgust. He abhors anything which lacks the creative function. Behind his tortured eyes is a man who patiently waits for an opportunity to inflict cruel revenge. A passing cloud of acid rain sprinkles brief acerbic showers onto the building. The side of the flats peel and corrode. Wisely he hides in a passageway until it is over.

—Just a little acid cloud! That won't keep me away you bastard of the night!

I still don't know who he expects to reply. Mr Nazarenko and I share a knowing smile.

Moosejaw Frontier

The Professor has exhausted himself. But he's far from finished. He has a routine. In summer the birch trees have hidden most of the detached village houses, so he'll continue his pursuit down there. The stalker always checks the flats then the woods first before entering Pope St Winter Street. We sit cramped, shoulder to shoulder, observing his behavior, making up dialogue for him, using him as a prop in our fictional games . . .

Chris Kelso

THE APOLOGY *(meta-pology)*

Yes, this is an apology. From me to you. An apology for everything which has gone before. If you've managed to stay with me this far, not only do I owe you an apology, I owe you a firm and friendly handshake (Yes I know I also owe you the £8 you misguidedly spent buying this book too, but I'll get to that—promise . . .). Perhaps the reason my characters elude me so much, and on such a regular basis, is because I myself am an unrealised character. "Dear diary . . . " eh? Well, I'm not attributing this all to youth but I feel like I owe you all an excuse of sorts (amongst all the other things I owe!).

According to scholars, (ie: NOT me), self-reflection has become the dominant subject of postmodern fiction.

All those nasty critics of postmodern metafiction claim that it marks the death of the novel as a genre, but I would argue that it signals the novel's resurrection. Literature as a medium, like music and art and cinema, has become stale, stale as an unused Durex in my wallet. Like the Durex's staleness, the death of all originality (with regard to plot, character and certain other dynamics) was also inevitable. Literature has suffered in a way similar to how music has suffered—it consists of only 12 notes and so, of course, we're going to start treading familiar ground eventually! If I wanted to be a writer I had to be one of those people who tried something new, even if the cash waited behind a different, more obvious door. I mean, who the fuck wants to make money??

138

Truth is, I cannot write mainstream fiction, nor can I adhere to any of its conventions. Sorry. *If On a Winter's Night a Traveler*, the 1979 novel by the Italian writer Italo Calvino, the narrative is about someone trying to read a book of the same name. Calvino is stalking about objectivity from the writer's point of view. I don't think there is any way I could completely remove myself from the process of writing a book and allow these characters to flourish into some independent construct. I have a great deal of respect for authors who are able to achieve this, who can imagine the blueprints for a character and then the rest is like dictation. This theme of a writer's objectivity is also explored in Calvino's *Mr. Palomar*, which, again, explores if absolute objectivity is possible. For me—it is not. That's why Juan escaped me, and continues to escape me . . .

This is more of a confessional than an actual apology. It's not my intention to justify my motives here. This is really more like therapy. In a sense this is probably the most selfish book ever written. Not only have I inflicted awkward themes (of subjectivity of meaning associated with post-structuralism) and the relationship between fiction and life on the reader, I am now **using** you (where I had previously promised an apology) as an armchair psychiatrist. For that I *can* offer you a sincere apology. Not.

This manuscript was completely undrafted. It all came out in one big splurge. Occasionally I brought patches of other dormant writing in, but generally it was shat into existence in one big clump. Therefore, it is a complete reflection of me. If I'm anything, I'm honest.

139

You don't always get such naked and authentic portrayals of a writer as you do here, no-siree—which is why I do not believe that I am a writer by nature, not truly.

Many postmodern metafictions are regarded by critics as representative of the "paranoid style,"—well that's completely true in my opinion. Because this is such a frank expression of me and my various paranoia's, metafiction was the only sensible style I could employ. I read *Lunar Park* by Brett Easton Ellis and loved it, I thought *"well if a writer as renowned as Ellis can write about himself and get away with it, then by Jove so can I!"*, but then I remembered 2 things.

- *The first was that Brett Easton Ellis was already a famous author; I was not (and never will be).*

- *The second thing I realised was that he was kind of a douche, at least in the eyes of the public.*

Maybe writing in this style wouldn't be the best move for me, after all, those who know me are aware that I'm a quiet and affable enough individual—but it was after reading *The Private Memoirs and Confessions of a Justified Sinner* by James Hogg, that I started thinking I could really get away with it. Hogg's brief cameo role in the final pages of the novel is his "signature" attached to the otherwise anonymous original publication. It would allow my writing to be self-conscious, introspective, introverted, narcissistic and auto-representational. As a self-absorbed creative person I jumped for joy. I'd found a loop hole! I could be a real writer without having to care about anyone but myself. Jane Austin mentions writing the novel by her narrator in *Northanger Abbey*. Miguel Cervantes' fifteenth century novel, *Don Quixote* did it. Jerry Seinfeld did it too. Hamlet references acting in Shakespeare's *Hamlet*. So Chris Kelso would do it . . .

The definition of the novel itself "notoriously defies definition", according to Patricia Waugh anyway. Waugh argues that *"contemporary metafictional writing is both a response and a contribution to an even more thoroughgoing sense that reality or history are provisional: no longer a world of external verities but a series of constructions, artifices, impermanent structures"*

Scholars like Ann Jefferson might dispute this.

By covertly baring and allowing complete access to all the fictional and linguistic systems I used, by having intertextual references (examining fictional systems like the Slave State/incorporating aspects of both theory and criticism/creating imaginary writers/creating fictional works for these imaginary character), I could let a conceited narrative metamorphosis the creative process into a wholly unique interpretative experience. The entire novel is an open trajectory where even the author himself questions his motives during the writing process.

But hell, I'm only 25, there's time for me to stop being such a pretentious wanker yet. There's time for me to write a proper book with characters you care about and a plot that ropes you in.

Isn't there? . . .

That peculiar smell of Granola and spices
Those strange dark clouds swelling overhead
The feel of buried bone beneath the hot sand
Sounds of a sinister marketplace where souls are bought and sold
The idle chit-chat of hungry monsters in cages
The howl of wind tearing through each and everyone's heart
Juan knew he'd arrived . . .

He saw the bar from the hotel window. A neon sign burning through the shadowy empire of hell—TITS AND BOOZE. Juan slid on his coat and headed to the bar leaving the hotel door wide open.

On the street-side was a woman Juan recognised. She was wearing a donkey mask and squatting over a rusty bucket. He didn't stop to check how he knew her. The woman's maternal familiarity set his teeth on edge. He barged through a cluster of immaculate yuppies on their cell phones, all wearing the same mask as the woman.

-What's tha' hurry?—Asked one yuppies, snorting through a large nostril and kicking dirt behind him with one large hind hoof.
- TITS AND BOOZE! He replied in feverish haste.

A spark of excitement danced down his spine as Juan drew closer to the bar. The humid air made breathing difficult but he was driven by an insane desire deep within himself.

The marketplace was busy with ghouls and

wailing souls trapped in Gherkin jars. Juan saw a familiar man browsing over a stand of buyable body parts. He had a strange contortion of pleasure on his face as the stall owner dug a candy scoop into a load of fingertips and shovelled them into a bag for him.

- Assalaamu Alaikum, I love the smell of Salaam in the mornin'—the owner said.

The familiar face took the bag and disappeared into the blackness. A fear of being castrated sank an anchor of nausea in Juan's gut.

The destination was close, he knew it.

Almost there.

Juan could smell the beer; practically feel the pink mounds of a lap dancing broad beneath the open palms of his hands. Virtually feel the hateful penis envying stares . . .

The clouds parted and rain descended. Still the thick humidity hung in the air like radioactive smog. Juan had to piss. He went to relieve himself behind one of the stalls. Once the stream began to flow, Juan saw a young boy he recognised.

He had dirty blonde hair

So did Juan

He had a mole on his upper lip

So did Juan

He spoke with a lazy S and his eyes sparkled in gunmetal grey . . .

You get the picture . . .

- I don't like you, said the boy.
- Good, I never liked you either, Juan replied, shaking the last of his piss out. The boy's face twisted and he began wailing.
- This is so typical of you, accused Juan, shaking a long adult sized index in the boy's agonised face. The rain stopped. He noticed a large damp stain cover over the boy's pants.

He finally reached the watering hole.

—TITS AND BOOZE—

Juan burst through the bar door barely able to contain his excitement. But his hopes were dashed when he realised the bar was empty. There was no bar, no waiter, no pool table, no tables or chairs but most alarmingly—no tits or booze! The bar wasn't a bar at all, but an empty warehouse. He heard a whimpering child facing the corner. That familiar man who wanted him castrated had removed his donkey mask. He had no face. He stared at Juan with an expressionless slab of pink flesh. Those familiar women who both aroused him and made him feel peaceful as a child were there too, equally blurred of any distinctive physiognomy.

Like the seedy motel, Juan was faced with the familiar sound of an empty room.

146

Outside, he could hear and smell the same things he'd always heard and smelled.

That peculiar smell of Granola and spices
Those strange dark clouds swelling overhead
The feel of buried bone beneath the hot sand
Sounds of a sinister marketplace where souls are bought and sold
The idle chit-chat of hungry monsters in cages
The howl of wind tearing through each and everyone's heart.

- Aren't you going to take off that mask Juan, it's hardly kosher?—came a voice he scarcely recognised.

Juan knew he'd arrived . . .

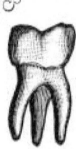

Bizarro Pulp Press Previews

Samples from some of our other books

ALL ART IS JUNK
BY R.A. HARRIS

Chapter 1

The dry heaving pipes of the dead jet pack sucking cold air sound like a low blood sugar level orchestra playing a piss poor staccato symphony, a hive of electronic farts played in super-slowmo. I press the ignition button repeatedly, the spark a strobing star, but there's no fuel for it to catch and ignite. The sun grins over the horizon behind us. We begin to descend, a sentient cymbal crescendo swan diving towards the final note of a fractured cadence. Scanning for a viable landing zone confirms presupposition. We aren't supposed to survive this one. This is the end of the tour.

Beneath us is a square mile island, most of it coated in a cruel blaze, mockingly eating the fuel we desperately need to keep us aloft. Beyond the flames the ocean beats the coast senseless from all sides, jagged waves curling over sagging rock dragging yet more land to the merciless deep. Men, foolish enough to venture that they were sailors, slap like landed fish against the rubble of their ships piled in Gimp Cove, the current pinning the vestiges to the edge of the land.

A thick shadow, thicker than even the heaviest rain cloud could muster, covers us as a teetering salmon flesh pink tower curls over us from behind. A giant finger rising from the ground come to squash us like a pest. Only this finger is made of hundreds of human bodies stacked like Jenga blocks, all elbows and knees and teeth grinding and flaking. As it leans in towards us, I sense her. She's there in the stack, almost anonymous amongst the mess of limbs and torsos jerking and swimming in the air trying to right the massive pink pillar, save it from face planting into the flaming ground. I thought our connection would have died by now but I recognize her trace signature. It's in my code. The tower swings back the other way, unveiling the morning sun, white light expanding like a ray gun blast. I turn and watch as the column sways back and forth like a comedic waiter carrying a tray of dishes containing jelly. Super zoom in to see her squawking face, cheeks stretched white like stressed plastic. Packed into the human skyscraper, a victim crushed in a gangbang orgy.

I've found Lana at last. She's become one of the totems. As we slowly cascade down towards the burning ground I throw the spare life ring I held onto towards her. It falls short as the flesh tower block bends away from us. Some opportunists further down the pile grab hold instead, anchoring us to the towering populace. We swing like Tarzan and Jane towards it. The screams of our landing zone are cut short by my steel feet smashing through pathetic skull bones like bricks through windows. I grasp onto spare limbs, using all my strength, causing the brittle bones to crumble like shortcrust pastry in my grip, strawberry sauce squirting out. We swing in a fancy arc away from the broken bodies, a lead pendulum balloon. The anchor slips and arms pulled from sockets come hurtling towards us as blood rains down, painting us ruby red. I sever the last of my laserwire to release the ring, and it spins away like an Olympic discus.

"What the fuck is going on?" Cilia has woken up. Her usual chipper self replaced by the semi-conscious demon princess strapped to my back, shocked back to life by a defibrillator in the form of freshly amputated limbs slapping her in the face.

"We are rapidly descending towards the Earth," I tell her, "and the ground is on fire."

"Then fucking deploy the crash landing gear according to protocol," she rips. A mechanical distorted oscillation tells me she has returned to snoozing immediately.

She is logical almost to a fault. I deploy the crash landing gear according to protocol without resistance: I press the CLP switch, ejecting the empty jet pack from my back and releasing seven thousand liters of compressed whipped cream from the emergency canister, it coats the Earth like a bukkake scene. The swarming fire melts most of it by the time we smack into the ground. The remaining cream doesn't slow our velocity even one iota and the soft ground swallows us like we're a bullet fired down a well.

Cilia remains rock-like in her sleep. The morning sky peeks in through the entrance to our cavity, a perfect Junk and Cilia shape some two hundred meters above, an angel bird in flight made of sleepy orange steadily blushing blue. Rain drops decanter onto Cilia's sensor, deforming the world.

The ground shakes violently as a thousand drums

steam roll art on top of us, burying us deep and dirty in the bowels of The Installation.

Chapter 2

The drum had been a constant since the deluge. A wild discordant beast, atemporal and offbeat. A chainsaw revolving at 0.01 rpm or there abouts, decay reverberating like a gunshot on the moors. The moment after Lana disappeared it became my death knell, signifying my grave was being dug in soft ground. A keeper without his quarry was as useful as a chocolate fireguard. A redundancy of metal and flesh, true to my name.

I was ingested by a jungle of people that grew about me as they spilled from the only nightclub on the island, their breath and cognition fermented. I began asking in earnest if they had seen Lana: she had somehow slipped the noose. Jaundiced faces lit by flickering torch and sinewy moonlight, escorted on bow legs and twisting feet, blankly gazed into my sensor as if looking at a rock or modern art installation. That drum spasm lashing like a whip occasioned a punctuation mark on my inquiry. Within moments the crowd had dispersed and I was left alone, regurgitated and holding the laserwire that should have been connecting me to Lana limply in my rusted hands. The last fifteen years of successfully fulfilling my sole task had effectively been negated in a single moment. A discontinuity, a blip, a segment of ruin deleting the previous data storage one and a half decades long, enough to fill ten landfill sites over.

Then, a colossal clang that set my clocks back to zero and violently shook connectors out of their ports ripped through the air. I immediately set my EM scanner to infrared, looking for the trademark balloon of white heat outlined in the tangerine orange of an explosion, but there was nothing amiss: the surrounding area was as cold as ever, a quiet purple hue, steady and calm, the wavering orange warmth of the crowd dissipating—leaving me, a lonely cloud. Soon, the only heat was in my head, like I'd been baptized in fire. It was a shameful heat, red blooded and clammy, melting my circuits, confusing and overloading my primary processors. I blew out smoke rings, red hot copper wire vaporized in my cheeks. I immediately blamed the laserwire. Antiquated technology from before The Installation.

I remember bringing the error in choosing such a connecting tissue up with Jessica, Lana's deceased mother. "Physical connections are ancient. Technology lets us communicate to each other through immaterial waves now, Jessica," I told her.

"If you can't feel each other how can you tell when you aren't in contact any more, Lancelot?" She implored me with glinting eyes, the same her daughter used on me in times of disagreement. The kind I wish Cilia would use, rather than her hacksaw tongue and razor wit. "I would feel so much more secure knowing she was bound to you by your strong grip. Besides, the laserwires today are supposed to be stronger than spiderweb a meter thick."

She had stumped me. I couldn't be sure how I would know we were still in contact without that physical tension between us. I might be receiving ghost messages, merely phantom exchanges created by a subconscious part of my server and looped back to me via a hidden circuit. It wasn't my place to second-guess my mistress either. After all, she was the human. I acquiesced and held tightly onto the laserwire, immediately falling in love with the calming series of baby-innocent thoughts pulsing brightly like a new born star.

Retracing my steps seemed the logical things to do. I must have waylaid her inside the club. I figured she was still at the bar, waiting for her ward to return. There's no way Mansell would have gotten to her already.

GRAVITY COMICS MASSACRE
BY VINCENZO BILOF

PROLOGUE AND EPILOGUE

Skinning was hard work, especially when the victim was still alive, although that didn't make it any less fun. Damien regretted he hadn't been able to find a woman for a long time. He preferred the tall, slender middle-class women who felt their futures were secure. They were fun to chop into pieces because even until their last breath, they still believed someone was going to save them.

He didn't particularly care for torture, but today, he was in the mood for it. The little Indian boy who'd been left for drunk on the side of the road by his buddies was in for one hell of a time, but at the very least, Damien would get what he wanted. The kid would experience one of his wildest dreams—in the flesh, of course.

Currently, the teenager sniveled and sobbed under duct tape, choking with his red, runny eyes focused intently on the fat man. Damien had no illusions about his weight issue—his mother told him once long ago that people would always find a way to judge him because of his size. So, it was best to embrace his physical 'deformity.' The truth of the matter was that

157

most people didn't understand how lucky he really was to have so much flesh.

Damien never cared much for clothes, even when his comic store was still open. Folds of fat jiggled over his soiled underwear, while a forest of hair on his thighs and chest curled in a swampy disaster of sweat and dirt. Damien stomped around the dusty, old store with a pen in his hand, habitually running his fingers along his hair.

"This is always so exciting," he stopped in front of the man and squeezed his hands together. "You see, Mr. Grayson—I'm going to call you that—um, well, this is an opportunity for you. When I started doing this, I had a lot of help. I wasn't quite sure what I wanted, so it was a bit messy. Now I know *exactly* what I want, and that makes this a whole lot easier for both of us. I usually only chop up women, but for everyone else, they get something a lot more special."

Mr. Grayson screamed against the duct tape.

Damien burst with a sudden laugh. "What the hell is your problem? It's not really that big of a deal! You see this pen in my hand? There's a story behind this pen. Now, you're sitting in the finest comic book store in the state of Arizona. It's the one attraction this shitty town has."

Damien gestured at the empty, cobwebbed shelves of *Gravity Comics,* and the windows caked with grime and some yellow, un-nameable substance that had been smeared across the glass. Meager light penetrated that wall of detritus and rot—just enough to reveal the cowering Indian boy who'd been unlucky enough to have wandered off his reservation with a bunch of friends and left on the side of the road as a joke.

"They had their eyes on me for a long time." Damien began to recount the tale, as he always liked to do. He had a flair for the dramatic; it was very likely he was previously incarnated as Edgar Rice Burroughs, or in the very least, Marlon Brando. He was a storyteller and an artist, but for most of his life, he'd been misunderstood.

"My mother knew them very well, you see. These friends of ours used to come and visit regularly, and they eventually explained they were the ones who inspired Stan Lee, and Phillip K. Dick. You know who I'm talking about, right?"

Grayson, of course, found it difficult to respond.

Damien sighed. "Fucking, Christ. I hate ignorance. I really do. And you know what? I'm not a big fan of torture, because it's *so* boring. It's overdone! You're expecting torture, aren't you? You're sitting there, pissing yourself, and you think I'm a sick fuck who's going to torture you. Well, guess what, Dick Grayson! Torture's fucking BO-RING. But you . . . YOU! I'm thinking about it. I really am. Only, I'm not all that good. I don't know anatomy or anything, so I might kill you before I'm actually done. That would piss me off."

Damien paced back and forth in an attempt to restart his story. "I was talking about the aliens. They were also the ones who helped write a bunch of religious stuff, too, but we're not here to talk about that garbage! I mean, I don't get it! How can you believe in God and not believe in aliens?"

Damien had been pacing back and forth. He sharply turned to face Mr. Grayson, and roared, "Did you hear WHAT I SAID? HOW CAN YOU BELIEVE IN GOD AND NOT ALIENS? Have you been listening? Aliens are behind everything! They're the ones who created all our favorite superheroes! So they were responsible for the success of my store, in a way. It was their idea in the first place. I grew up with these aliens, and they have a name, but that's too complicated for you. I can see I'm already over your head."

Damien pulled up a chair opposite his prey, scraping it against the floorboards that had been stripped of bloodstained carpet long ago. He drooled into the forest of curly, black hair on his chest while retrieving his clipboard from the counter. He sat his bulbous body down into the chair.

"I'll do the work," he grumbled to himself. "They want their data, after all. Don't worry about me, I can see just fine. I promise we won't be interrupted. My friends have done all they can to separate us from the rest of the world. Nobody will come for you because they can't see us! Not detectable by satellites, visible only to the naked eye. Speaking of eyes . . . " Damien's tone became introspective and professorial, like a professor of literature poring over a graphic novel while attempting to discern its educational value. "I wonder what goes on when you close yours? What're your nightmares like, Mr. Grayson? Tell me about them, but don't do it with your lips. Allow me to watch you squirm as your worst fear comes true. It's not for me to know, but you see, my liege lords require data to help them continue with their analysis of the human psyche. They require your fear, and in exchange, I get to decorate my wondrous store."

With the pen that his benefactors gave him, he began to sketch out a rough draft of the unfortunate young man. Damien didn't know exactly how the pen worked, only that the device could make a man realize his fears. Whatever horrible sensations Mr. Grayson envisioned awaited him; the data was crucial to the success of the benign experiment. It didn't matter what the experiment was; Damien was fulfilling his destiny.

Damien was an excellent artist; he should have been drawing comics for DC ages ago, but they didn't realize how talented he was.

He sucked drool into his mouth while studying the writhing victim. When the drawing was finally finished, he retrieved his toolbox and brought it into the room. It was time to wallpaper the room.

The Indian boy dreamed.

***

Cheveyo sat on the worn couch in the trailer where he lived with his mother, three sisters, and grandmother. Any minute now, his boys would be coming to pick him up for a night at the bar. Rosie the bartender was working tonight. He pretended to be confident in front of his friends that she would eventually capitulate to his advances. He wrote her poems and bought her flowers, but she kept up her snide remarks—poured his shots with a smirk on her face while she listened to him rant about how beautiful she was. At least she was always nice enough to call a cab whenever his friends ditched him.

Out of the corner of his eye, a flash of movement skittered across the threadbare carpet. A trick of perception, nothing more. He continued to play with his smart phone, checking for a text message from one of his buddies because they were running late. More movement to his peripheral prompted him to turn again and scan the floor. No one was in the trailer but him. The room's silence allowed him to feel the speed of his heartbeat. He returned his gaze to the barren land outside the window, and only a moment later, he glimpsed a shape race across the floor and disappear beneath the sofa.

Cheveyo felt ridiculous. Tiny creatures or objects that moved quickly reminded him of spiders, and his sensitivity to arachnophobia often had him look away from shadowy corners. Spiders could easily hide in dirty, dusty environments that were rarely touched by human hands. Looking beneath the sofa was hardly an attractive proposition, but it was the only way to stop his heart's incessant hammering. Rosie knew he had a fond distaste for spiders and often made jokes about his weakness.

It was time to 'man-up' and get his shit together. Rosie would want a strong man, not a little piss-ant who was afraid of creepy crawlies.

He took a deep breath and leaned over the edge of the couch to peer underneath.

At first, they looked like furry hands. Cheveyo stopped breathing. Reality seemed to have paused. His brain processed the black stripes across the long, spindly legs. He blinked. He blinked again. And again. A million eyes stared back at him from the fissure between the couch and the floor. He wanted to move, but his body wouldn't respond. He couldn't hear anything but Rosie's voice in his head, calling him a pussy.

He curled up into a ball on the corner of the couch. His hands closed into tight balls that he couldn't open, his fingertips cold, his lips unmoving. He couldn't tear his eyes away from the edge of the cushions; he waited. He tested his sanity and waited while his eyelids refused to fall. It would have been better to look away, to tell himself that it wasn't real, but his entire body was held in stasis, and all sensation was terminated. He couldn't feel the cold fingertips anymore, and his heartbeat faded as blood rushed to his head and filled his ears.

The first flesh-colored arachnid trickled over the sagging middle cushion. It moved slowly and deliberately. It spanned the width of a man's hand. Stopping in the middle of the couch, it might have been staring at him, fearlessly judging him as a meek creature. The spider climbed over the top, and Chevyo wanted to follow it with his eyes; his fragmented consciousness demanded a course of action. He should retrieve a weapon, or run, or wake the FUCK UP. But it was no use.

His lips parted only slightly to allow a shallow exhalation that should have been a scream.

Another spider, a twin to the first, rambled over the floor toward the sofa. Two more followed after it. Several more emerged from beneath the sofa and blanketed its surface, creating a forest of fuzzy legs. They were silent and watchful, methodically creeping over the upholstery.

Cheveyo didn't feel the piss that filled the crotch of his jeans. His neck unfroze, and he turned only slightly to see his cell phone vibrate against the floor. His friends were calling—everything was normal, after all. He sighed and closed his eyes. The spiders weren't real. Maybe he was an alcoholic, and he was starting to hallucinate as the result of shitty withdrawal symptoms. At the very least, this was just a bad dream . . . a bad dream . . .

He opened his eyes again when he felt something jerking on his pant leg, imploring him to pay attention. He watched as hundreds of hand-sized, tiger-striped spiders crawled over the ceiling and along the walls. His bowels loosened completely, and his pants filled up.

One of them climbed over his leg and perched atop his knee cap.

Cheveyo finally screamed, though no one could hear him.

ALL ART IS JUNK

Lana Rivers, a girl with paintbrush hair, is missing and it's up to Lancelot, her cyborg knight, and his bionic conjoined twin, Cilia, to find her before her evil father, a disrespected artist turned mad-scientist, performs a terrible experiment on her.

WWW.BIZARROPULPPRESS.COM

FECAL TERROR

A killer turd is on the loose!

WWW.BIZARROPULPPRESS.COM

THE AFTER-LIFE STORY OF PORK KNUCKLES MALONE

What's a farm boy to do when his pet pig becomes an evil, decaying hunk of ham with slime-spewing psychic powers?

NOTES FROM THE GUTS OF A HIPPO

A rugged journalist by the name of Jay Robbins is sent on a mission to the dangerous jungles of Brazil to search for a missing hippopotamus researcher and a news story. Along the way, he stumbles upon a mythical breed of hippo, the Lastir, which harbors another world within its guts and secrets he could only imagine. It won't be easy though. With two elderly assassins trailing him and a bunch of notes, Robbins has his job cut out for him.

Lightning Source UK Ltd.
Milton Keynes UK
UKHW011841130223
416874UK00001B/319